"You and Buzz nee
back bedroom. Now. Lock the doors,
and don't come out until I tell you."

Colton pulled out the gun from his waistband, his jaw set with steely determination.

Sarah didn't argue. She scrambled away, hardly able to breathe.

But as she locked the door, Buzz beside her, she pressed her ear there, trying to hear what was going on.

It was silent as Colton waited, seeming to prepare himself for battle.

Sarah waited. The moments felt like hours.

Flashbacks from earlier hit her, making her flinch. Images of seeing that man in Loretta's room. Watching as Loretta took her last breath.

Now Colton was in danger.

She stood and pressed herself into the wall, resisting the urge to look out the window and see what was going on.

She didn't have to.

She heard tires crunching on gravel in the distance.

Someone was here.

Christy Barritt's books have won a Daphne du Maurier Award for Excellence in Suspense and Mystery and have been twice nominated for an RT Reviewers' Choice Best Book Award. She's married to her Prince Charming, a man who thinks she's hilarious—but only when she's not trying to be. Christy is a self-proclaimed klutz, an avid music lover and a road-trip aficionado. For more information, visit her website at christybarritt.com.

TRAINED TO DEFEND

CHRISTY BARRITT

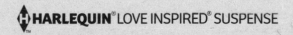

HARLEQUIN® LOVE INSPIRED® SUSPENSE

If you purchased this book without a cover you should be aware
that this book is stolen property. It was reported as "unsold and
destroyed" to the publisher, and neither the author nor the
publisher has received any payment for this "stripped book."

Recycling programs
for this product may
not exist in your area.

LOVE INSPIRED BOOKS

ISBN-13: 978-1-335-40254-7

Trained to Defend

Copyright © 2020 by Christy Barritt

All rights reserved. Except for use in any review, the reproduction
or utilization of this work in whole or in part in any form by any
electronic, mechanical or other means, now known or hereafter
invented, including xerography, photocopying and recording, or in
any information storage or retrieval system, is forbidden without
the written permission of the editorial office, Love Inspired Books,
195 Broadway, New York, NY 10007 U.S.A.

This is a work of fiction. Names, characters, places and incidents are
either the product of the author's imagination or are used fictitiously, and
any resemblance to actual persons, living or dead, business establishments,
events or locales is entirely coincidental.

This edition published by arrangement with Love Inspired Books.

® and TM are trademarks of Love Inspired Books, used under license.
Trademarks indicated with ® are registered in the United States Patent
and Trademark Office, the Canadian Intellectual Property Office and in
other countries.

www.Harlequin.com

Printed in U.S.A.

God is our refuge and strength, a very present help in trouble. Therefore will not we fear, though the earth be removed, and though the mountains be carried into the midst of the sea; Though the waters thereof roar and be troubled, though the mountains shake with the swelling thereof.
—*Psalm* 46:1-3

This book is dedicated to Rusty, Sparky, Molly and Buttons. My furry companions are faithfully by my side every day as I sit down to write. Thanks for the inspiration and letting me be your person.

ONE

Sarah Peterson quietly opened the back door to her new, temporary home in Spokane, Washington, and slunk inside. The warm glow of delight spread inside her as she reflected on her evening. Maybe things were finally starting to look up for her.

She'd been at an art show this evening, and two people had shown interest in her work. All she needed was one big break, and maybe all of the hardship of these past several years could finally be in her past—and stay there.

Behind her, the freezing rain pounded relentlessly as a mid-January storm claimed the area. Forecasters had predicted the precipitation would soon turn to snow and conditions outside would become perilous.

But now, inside the house, everything around Sarah was dark and quiet with the stillness of the evening.

Good. Loretta must be sleeping.

And, if Sarah was smart, she'd remain quiet so the woman could continue sleeping.

Loretta Blanchard wasn't the type of woman you wanted to wake up—or even look at the wrong way, for that matter. She was a force to be reckoned with, and if she didn't like you, she would make your life miserable.

Sarah left her damp coat on a hanger by the door in

order not to track any water inside. As she crept through the kitchen, she looked around for Buzz, Loretta's emotional support dog. The husky always greeted her at the door.

Strange. Where was he?

Buzz was one of Sarah's favorite parts about this job. She'd never met an animal with such intelligent eyes, and his wagging tail was just the welcome she needed on most days. Her muscles tightened as she wondered where the dog was.

Sarah headed through the dark house toward her bedroom so she could change out of her dress and heels. Her bag slid from her shoulder as she slipped her heels off and carried them up the massive staircase.

Her boss was a scientific genius who'd created a new medication to help people with arthritis. She'd been at the top of her game until ALS, also known as Lou Gehrig's disease, had claimed her body and weakened her muscles. However, her mind was just as sharp as ever.

Sarah stepped into her room, flipped on the light and paused.

Something felt off.

Her spine tightened, and she glanced around her room. Everything appeared in place. Her ivory quilt was neat. Her curtains were drawn. Her dresser drawers closed.

But something was different. She was sure of it.

Her mom had always said that Sarah had an eye and an ear for detail. It was probably what made her such a good artist today. She noticed things that others didn't. Slivers of light hidden beneath barren trees. A shy bird singing among the throng of boisterous ones. The way the sky still turned different colors for nearly an hour after the sunset.

So what had alerted her senses that something was wrong right now?

Sarah's eyes went to the closet. Was someone in there?

She grabbed the scissors from her dresser. She'd used them to trim her bangs this morning. Holding them like a knife, she stepped closer to the door.

Her lungs froze as she reached for the knob.

This was probably nothing.

Dear Lord, please don't let this be a mistake.

After lifting the silent prayer, she jerked the door open.

Something leaped toward her. Sarah swallowed a scream and threw herself back.

An oversize ball of fur nearly knocked her off her feet.

Buzz.

Buzz?

As the dog pounced on her, Sarah rubbed his head, sensing something was wrong—desperately wrong. "Why are you in my closet, boy? And you've been so quiet."

Buzz whined.

The only reason he'd be in her closet was if Loretta put him there and commanded him to stay, Sarah realized. But if Loretta, who was in a wheelchair, had gone through all of that trouble, she had to have a really good reason. There was an elevator in the house, but Loretta hated using it.

Buzz whined again, trying to tell her something.

"What is it, boy?" Sarah murmured, leaning toward the canine.

Her words seemed to give the dog permission. He charged toward her bedroom door, nuzzled it open and ran into the hallway. Still gripping the scissors, Sarah took off after him.

The dog ran down the stairs and toward the opposite wing of the house—the wing where Loretta's bedroom was located.

"Buzz!" Sarah whispered, urgency lacing her voice.

She didn't want the dog to wake up Loretta. Then again, maybe Buzz knew something she didn't.

She swallowed hard at the thought.

Sarah didn't have much time to think. No, she could barely keep up with Buzz.

She caught sight of the dog as he pushed his way into Loretta's bedroom and disappeared.

The knot in her stomach squeezed tighter.

This wasn't like Buzz. The dog was usually regal and reserved.

A groan emerged from the darkness, then a loud, hard crash.

Something was wrong. Really wrong.

Sarah flung herself into Loretta's room, fully expecting to find Loretta having a medical emergency of some sort. She froze in the doorway and gasped.

A masked man stood over Loretta as she lay on the floor, her wheelchair shoved to the side.

Fear rippled through Sarah.

What was going on here?

The intruder glanced over at Sarah—but only for a second—before Buzz charged at him and knocked him off Loretta and into the wall. The man's head hit the wall.

The man groaned before his eyes closed and his body went limp. Had he lost consciousness?

Either way, Buzz still growled on top of him.

With her heart beating out of control, Sarah's gaze slid across the room and stopped at Loretta.

She moaned on the floor, her chest rising and falling too quickly. Rapid gasps sounded at her parted lips.

Sarah hurried toward her, kneeling at her side. Blood gushed from a puncture wound in the woman's neck.

Tears rushed to Sarah's eyes. That man had hurt her. She and Buzz had gotten here too late.

"Loretta, hold on," Sarah whispered, grasping her boss's shoulders. "I'll call 911. Help will be here soon."

"Sarah…" Loretta's voice was so faint that Sarah could hardly understand it.

The woman tried to sit up, but Sarah gently pushed her back down. She was in no condition to move right now.

"It's okay," Sarah said. "Just stay still."

Loretta's sixty-year-old face wrinkled with pain that whispered across every feature, a face that had only recently developed fine lines. The woman was always so strong. Seeing her like this…

It made Sarah's heart twist into knots.

"You've…got…to…go," Loretta rasped.

"No, I need to stay here with you." A shiver went up Sarah's spine as she said the words. There was more at stake here than just Loretta's wound.

The man who'd done this to her was still in the room. Still passed out. For now.

But he could wake up at any time and try to finish what he'd started.

Loretta might be hurt, but her grip was strong as she grasped Sarah's arm. "Take…Buzz…and…run. Far away. Danger."

Her eyes closed. She was fading, Sarah realized. Near death. Delirious maybe.

Had Sarah understood her words correctly? Run? Why would she run? She needed to stay here with Loretta.

"Ms. Blanchard—"

The woman squeezed her arm again, her gaze coming alive with a spark of intensity. "Go. Now. He'll…kill you."

"What?" The breath left Sarah's lungs. Hearing the words out loud made a fresh round of panic swell in her.

"Don't…trust…the…police."

"But—" What did she mean? If she couldn't trust the police, then who could she trust?

Loretta's gaze suddenly locked on to Sarah's. "Buzz…"

"What about Buzz?"

"Take…him…"

Before she could finish her sentence, Loretta shut her eyes, and her grip loosened—went limp.

She was gone, Sarah realized.

"Oh, Loretta." Grief stabbed at Sarah. But she didn't have time to dwell on it. Urgency pushed her on.

That man was beginning to stir. His limbs jerked, and soon he'd be awake. She felt certain of it.

Sarah stood, dropping the scissors from her hands.

She needed to go. If Loretta had given her those instructions, there was a good reason. The woman was smart, and she must know something that Sarah didn't.

"Buzz, come on."

Looking back at the man in black one more time, Sarah tore through the house.

She and Buzz had to get out of here. Now.

And there was only one place she could think to go. However, it was the last place she wanted to be.

Colton Hawk froze as a strange sound pulled him from his sleep.

It was a car. Coming up the gravel lane that led to his home. At four thirty in the morning.

He jumped out of his warm bed and threw on some clothes. After grabbing the gun from his nightstand, he peered out the window. Adrenaline pounded through him.

Unexpected visitors in the middle of the night usually meant trouble.

As a former detective, Colton had a whole list of people who might want to track him down and exact revenge. Apparently, not even moving out here to ten acres in northern Idaho was enough to keep people away.

He watched as the driver cut the headlights as he neared the house. He didn't recognize the beat-up sedan. But the fact that the driver was being secretive set off all kinds of warning alarms in his mind.

Colton hurried down the stairs to his front door. He stepped out onto his porch just as the vehicle rolled to a stop behind his truck.

With his finger poised on the gun, Colton waited to see what would happen next.

Snow pelted down from above, and the darkness obscured the landscape around him. Nightfall out here in the middle of Idaho's Rocky Mountains was unlike any Colton had ever experienced. The blackness was so deep, a person felt like they could be swallowed by it.

The isolation was both a friend and a foe.

Colton knew one thing. someone had to be desperate to head out in slick, treacherous weather like this, especially in a sedan like the one in front of his house. The vehicle looked like it could break down at any minute. The front bumper was dented, the driver's side door was faded, and the tires looked tiny and worn down.

He glanced beyond the car to make sure no one else had followed. He saw nothing, no one—just a dark, empty lane lined with pine and fir trees.

Colton sucked in a breath when a dog hopped from the backseat and into the knee-high snow. A husky.

Why would someone bent on revenge have brought a dog with them?

And then he saw the biggest trouble of all.

Sarah Peterson stepped out and stared across the expanse at him.

He sucked in another breath.

Sarah. His Sarah.

Colton never thought he'd see the woman again, not after the way things had ended between them two years ago.

But there she was. Even in the darkness, he could see that she looked just as beautiful as ever with her shiny blond hair and petite figure. But something about her body language was different. Gone was the lighthearted, carefree vibe that Colton had loved so much. In its place was… terror. It was the only word he could think of to describe the look.

She staggered toward him and collapsed into the mounds of white, icy flakes that covered his front yard.

Colton jammed his gun into his waistband and rushed toward her. The dog barked at him, urging him on, telling him he wasn't moving fast enough.

When he reached Sarah, snow already encased her limp body.

She was…barefoot? In a knee-length dress?

What was going on? Why would she be dressed like this in such frigid weather? Something was seriously wrong.

Colton gathered her in his arms and carried her inside his house. Despite the craziness of the moment, he still caught of whiff of Sarah's honeysuckle-scented lotion.

At one time, it had been one of his favorite aromas in the world. It brought back memories of watching sunsets in each other's arms. Of dreaming about the future while hiking their favorite trail. Of good-night kisses and long hugs on the porch.

Shoving aside the bittersweet memories, Colton lowered Sarah onto his leather couch. She was freezing and had to warm up. He'd call an ambulance, but it would take twenty minutes to get here.

Before grabbing a blanket, his eyes skimmed the light

blue sweater covering her arms. Was that…blood on her sleeves?

Colton sucked in a breath.

What in the world had happened to her?

He quickly checked her for wounds but saw nothing. That meant the blood wasn't hers.

Wasting no more time, he grabbed a blanket and covered her. That blanket wouldn't be enough, though. He went to the fireplace and added wood, waiting until the blaze fanned and filled the room with more heat. Then he turned up his thermostat, hoping it kicked in quickly.

Colton went back to check on Sarah. He felt confident she just needed to warm up. He'd let her rest for a few minutes before deciding his next step.

His breath caught as he gazed at her. Beautiful Sarah.

He hadn't expected to see her again. Ever. Not after the way things had ended. Not after she'd chosen a job over a future with him. Bitterness tried to claw at him, but Colton pushed it away. There wasn't time for that now.

The dog nuzzled his hand, and Colton looked down at him. The husky sat directly in front of Colton, almost as if telling him that he had to answer to this canine.

"What happened, boy?" Colton murmured.

The dog let out a soft growl and stared at Sarah.

"Something bad, huh?" Colton's stomach tightened. If only the dog could speak.

Colton double-checked Sarah's vitals. Her pulse was good. She was breathing and didn't appear feverish.

She must have passed out from exhaustion or shock.

Lord, be with her. I don't know what happened, but I know she needs You now.

Just as he said "Amen," Sarah began thrashing on the couch, and her breathing quickened.

"He's coming," Sarah murmured, her eyes still closed. "He's coming."

Colton's back stiffened. Who was coming? What exactly had Sarah gotten herself mixed up in?

He didn't know. He only knew that the woman he'd once loved had somehow found herself in serious trouble.

TWO

Sarah jerked her eyes open and startled at the unfamiliar space around her.

Where was she? Was that man here—the man who'd killed Loretta? Had he caught Sarah and taken her somewhere?

She sprang up, swinging her gaze around as panic seized her. Movement caught the side of her vision.

The killer. He was here.

Sarah raised her hands, ready to give every last ounce of her strength to stay alive.

Her arm jerked toward him. But, before her fist connected with the man, he grabbed her wrists.

The action immobilized her. She thrashed, trying to get away. It was no use. The man…he was too strong. He overpowered her too easily.

"Sarah, it's okay." His voice sounded surprisingly calm and soothing—not at all like Sarah had imagined.

But she wouldn't let that fool her.

"No, it's not okay." With one last burst of strength, she began fighting again.

"Sarah, it's me. Colton."

Slowly, her ex-fiancé's face came into view.

Colton.

That was right. She'd fled to Colton's house. She barely remembered making it here.

She only vaguely recalled driving around as if on auto-pilot. Of deciding to come here but changing her mind. Of wandering country back roads in the dark, worried about running out of gas.

She remembered the panic. Remembered not thinking clearly.

As more details from last night flooded back to Sarah, she gasped.

Details about Loretta. Of the woman's final moments.

Tears sprang to her eyes, and her limbs shook uncontrollably.

Loretta was dead. She'd passed right there in Sarah's arms while her attacker had lain collapsed against the wall.

As Colton released her hands, Sarah leaned back, desperate to hold herself together. Yet she couldn't.

No, she'd been so frantic that she'd run to the very man who'd broken her heart—only he refused to acknowledge that he'd been the one to pull away. Colton refused to understand why Sarah had no choice but to leave, refused to understand that this was never about her art.

Buzz appeared beside Sarah, and his cold nose nuzzled her hand. She smiled and rubbed the dog's head, finding comfort in his familiar scent.

Her smile faded quickly.

Poor Buzz…he must feel worse than she did. Buzz had loved Loretta so much.

And now she was gone.

Another guttural cry escaped.

Colton leaned toward her, his gaze intense and concerned. "Sarah, you need to tell me what's going on."

She studied Colton a moment. Glanced at the perfect lines of his face. His messy light brown hair.

The man always got her pulse racing.

But he was off-limits. Sarah needed to remember that. He'd already broken her heart once. If he broke it again, she wasn't sure it could ever be repaired.

Which was why coming here had been such a horrible idea. Sarah definitely hadn't been thinking clearly. Otherwise, she would have gone anywhere else.

She gathered the blanket around her and stared at the fire in front of her. Buzz lay down beside her, his icy blue gaze on Colton, as if daring him to make one wrong move.

She needed to tell Colton why she was here. But first she needed to collect her thoughts. Besides, she wasn't sure she could say the words aloud.

Every time she remembered what happened it felt like a punch in her gut. Maybe this was a nightmare. Maybe she would wake up. Sarah wished those things might be true and, even more, she wished she believed them.

But she knew the truth. She just didn't know if she could find her voice long enough to share.

"Can I...can I have some tea?" Sarah asked, buying herself time. "Please. I... I just can't get warm."

As if on cue, her teeth chattered. The reaction had little to do with the cold, however. No, it felt like someone had rammed an icicle into her chest and shattered her emotions.

"Of course." Colton stood. "But then we need to talk."

Why *had* Sarah come here? Why couldn't she think of anywhere else she'd be safe?

She knew why. Colton had always been a protector. Even if he had been distant and withdrawn toward the end of their engagement, he was still, in some way, her safe place.

The drive here flashed back to her.

There had been headlights behind her. They'd appeared about fifteen minutes into her escape.

Sarah had tried to lose the driver, fearing it was the man who'd killed Loretta.

But what if she hadn't lost him?

She jumped to her feet and pulled the blanket around her as she walked toward the window. She had to know if she was truly safe here or not. Sarah had to see if anyone lingered outside, waiting to make his next move.

Buzz followed beside her, keeping a watchful eye on her.

"What are you doing?" Colton asked from across the open expanse of the room. His hands froze on the teakettle, as if he braced himself for action.

"That man…" Sarah started, fear seizing her again.

She couldn't get the image of Loretta's dying figure out of her mind. Couldn't forget the horror of finding that man standing over her.

"What man, Sarah?" Colton stepped from around the breakfast bar, coming toward her. "Who are you talking about?"

Sarah shook her head, battling the memories and hoping this was all a bad dream. She knew it wasn't. "I'm afraid… I'm afraid he followed me."

Colton took her elbow and led her back to the couch. "If that's the case, the last place you want to be is in front of the window."

She felt stoic as she sat back on the cushions and stared at the fire. The kettle whistled.

"One minute," he murmured. "Then we need to talk."

A moment later, Colton handed her some tea, complete with sugar and cream. He'd remembered what she liked. The thought shouldn't bring her so much delight.

"Sarah, you need to tell me what's going on." Colton stood with his hands on his hips. "Tell me why you have blood on your clothes."

At his words, she glanced down and gasped. He was right. Loretta's bloodstained her sweater.

A new round of tears welled up in her eyes. She jerked the sweater off, unable to stand the thought. She tossed it on the couch out of sight, wishing she could discard her memories as easily. But life didn't work that way.

Colton's intelligent, compassionate gaze remained latched on to hers. He sat on the chair near the couch, leaning toward her, waiting to listen.

He'd positioned himself at a place where he could also see the windows.

Sarah didn't miss that fact. Colton was always the cop, wasn't he? He was ever vigilant, kind of like Buzz.

She sucked in a deep, shaky breath. She wanted to forget about tonight. Erase it from her mind. Yet she realized that she couldn't do that. She was going to have to go back and revisit those dark moments.

As she opened her mouth, words wouldn't escape. "I…" Where did she even start?

"It's okay," Colton prodded. "What happened last night?"

She drew in a deep breath, praying for courage as she shared the truth. "I've been working for a woman, Loretta, and living in her home. I returned to her house last night and found her on the floor in her room. Bleeding." Her voice cracked.

Colton's eyes widened. "What happened next?"

"Buzz knocked out the man who attacked her. I tried to help Loretta, but she told me to take Buzz and run and to not trust the police. And then she…" Sarah swallowed hard. "Then she died. She was gone."

"I'm sorry, Sarah."

She nodded stiffly. "So, I did what she told me. I didn't know what else to do. I didn't even put my shoes on. I just… I wanted to get away."

"What happened to the man?"

"He was still in the house when I left. Buzz had jumped on him, and I think the man hit his head and was knocked unconscious. But then, on the way here, I was certain someone was following me."

Colton stiffened. "Why do you say that?"

Sarah shivered at the memories. "There were headlights. And they always seemed to be there, even when I turned off the main highway. I lost him… I think. I mean, I didn't see the car for the last thirty minutes of my trip."

"Why did you come here, Sarah?"

She swallowed hard, downing every last ounce of her pride as her gaze met Colton's. "Because I didn't know what else to do or who else I could trust. Please help me, Colton. Please."

Colton tried to process everything that Sarah had told him. He had so many questions but most of those could wait until later. Right now, he was concerned about Sarah. About how frail she looked. About how her arms trembled so badly she could hardly drink her tea.

"Sarah, I need to call the police—"

"No!" She nearly jumped off the couch, and Buzz followed her, standing on guard. "You can't. Loretta said not to."

"Why would she say that?" What sense did it make? The woman had been murdered. If Sarah had called the police, maybe the guy who'd committed the crime would be behind bars right now.

"I have no idea. But if she said it…she had a reason."

"But the police could catch this killer. Time is of the essence in situations like these and—"

Sarah glanced around, as if looking for her keys or purse or whatever she would have brought with her. "I should leave. I'm sorry. I shouldn't have come here. Some part of me thought I could trust you, though."

Colton touched her arm, ignoring the electricity that came from feeling her soft skin. "Don't leave. That's not what I'm saying. Please, sit down. We'll figure this out. I'm just asking questions right now."

She stared at him. Said nothing.

Finally, she nodded and lowered herself back onto the couch across from him. Buzz jumped up beside her and laid his head on her lap.

"Let's just talk." Colton spoke softly, trying to put her at ease and alleviate some of her caginess. "Okay?"

Sarah nodded, but her eyes looked strained and unconvinced. Instead, she leaned forward and rubbed Buzz's head.

"Do you have any idea why anyone would want Loretta dead?" he asked.

Sarah shook her head. "No. And…the more I think about it, the stranger it all is."

"Why do you say that?"

"Because I found Buzz locked in my closet upstairs. He couldn't have gotten himself locked in there. It wouldn't make any sense."

"Okay. You think Loretta put him there?"

"It's the only thing that makes sense. If the killer had put him there, Buzz would have been a wreck, clawing to get out. But he was sitting there obediently." As Sarah talked, she continued to rub the dog's head.

"So, he's well trained."

Sarah nodded. "That's right. But the thing is… Loretta could hardly get up the steps. She had ALS. If she went through all that trouble…"

"Then she suspected something might happen."

"Exactly." Sarah trembled again. "I don't know what's

going on, but I don't like it. I hope I didn't lead trouble here, Colton. I didn't think I was going to make it. The roads were so icy. And the drive was long and dark. I barely had enough gas. So many things were not in my favor."

"It sounds like God was watching over you to bring you this far," Colton said.

"I agree." Her gaze met his, her brief moment of gratefulness at their spiritual connection replaced by fear. "What am I going to do?"

"We'll figure something out, Sarah." Had he just said that?

Colton had taken time off from law enforcement, even though he'd been offered a job in investigative services with the Idaho State Police.

One day, he thought he might go back into that line of work. But, if he ever had hopes of doing that, the last thing he needed to do was harbor someone who might be wanted in a police investigation. And if the police weren't looking for Sarah yet, they would be soon.

Still, one look at Sarah, and Colton knew he couldn't refuse helping her. She'd always had that effect on him.

Sarah rubbed her hands against her dress and frowned. "Colton, is there a way you could… I don't know. Maybe call someone? Maybe use some of your connections to find out if there are any updates? Maybe the police caught this guy. Maybe those headlights I saw were just another traveler headed in the same direction I was. I just don't know. Nothing makes sense, and nothing will make sense until I have more answers."

He didn't say anything for a moment and instead sat there, letting her words settle.

She frowned. "I'm asking too much, aren't I? I'm sorry."

"I'll see what I can do," Colton finally said before nodding toward the hallway. "Listen, first, why don't you take a shower?"

"A shower sounds nice."

"I'll find you something to wear and you can leave what you have on now outside the door. I'll wash everything for you and leave you something fresh. Once you've cleaned up, we figure out a plan."

Sarah continued to stare at him, as if trying to gauge his thoughts, to figure out if he was still trustworthy. "You're not going to call the police while I'm in the shower, are you?"

"I won't. You know I'm as good as my word."

Finally, she nodded. "Okay then."

But just as she stood, her phone buzzed. She pulled it from her purse and looked at the screen. Her face went pale.

"What is it?" Colton moved closer, sensing something was wrong.

"It's a message…from Loretta."

The killer must have grabbed the woman's phone, Colton realized.

"What does it say?" Colton asked, glancing over her shoulder. As he read the words there, his blood went colder than an Idaho winter.

I know who you are, and I will find you. You have something I want.

THREE

Sarah's heart raced as she sat on the couch and stared at the words on her phone.

The killer knew who she was? How? What did this mean?

Fear rushed through her. Exactly what was this man planning to do when he found her? Sarah didn't even have to ask that question. She *knew* what he planned on doing.

He would kill her.

She should have pulled up his mask and looked at his face. At least then she would know what the man looked like.

But it was too late for that now. It didn't matter.

Her head spun as reality again hit her and left her reeling.

"It's going to be okay, Sarah," Colton said beside her.

His voice snapped her back to the moment. His platitude was meant to bring her comfort but it failed. Nothing was going to be okay. Nothing.

Why couldn't Colton see that? Why did he always think things would be okay when they clearly wouldn't? Sometimes people couldn't change their circumstances, no matter how hard they tried.

Sarah's life had been a case in point.

Nothing had gone the way she'd planned—including her relationship with Colton.

She put her hands over her face. Why had she ever come here? What had she been thinking?

This was just one more bad decision in a long line of them.

Colton leaned closer, still staring at her phone. As he did, his arm brushed hers, and a surge of old memories rushed through her. Memories of when life used to be happy. When the future had seemed bright. When it looked like her future wouldn't be a repeat of her past.

Sarah had been wrong then. As much as she wanted to believe and trust in God's plan for her future, she'd accepted the fact that her future was meant to be full of struggles. Other people might cruise through life and find happiness. But not Sarah.

Her father had left. Her mother had been arrested. She and her sister had grown up with a string of foster care families—and they hadn't been together in most of those homes.

No, life had never been smooth sailing. Even now as an adult, life had been full of financial and career struggles, all of which had led her to this point.

"Do you have any idea what he's talking about when he says, 'You have something I want'?" Colton asked, his gaze still laser focused on her phone screen and that text she'd received.

Sarah's mind raced, charging back to the present. What *did* the man mean? What exactly had he come to Loretta's to get this evening?

"I have no clue," she said, her voice shaky. "I left with nothing. All my things are still at Loretta's. It was just me and Buzz and a few of Buzz's essentials that were in a bag by the back door."

She leaned down and patted Buzz's head. The dog leaned into her, but Sarah noted how his eyes remained on guard as he scanned the room.

She felt sorry for Buzz. He'd cherished Loretta so much and had been such a faithful companion.

The dog was truly beautiful. White with gray spots. His eyes were an icy blue, and he had a matching collar. Despite his regal demeanor, the dog also had a playful side. Loretta had trained him well. All she had to do was cluck her tongue once, twice or three times, and he would immediately obey whatever command corresponded.

In fact, in some ways, the dog had been like a child to Loretta. Buzz had been raised to act as an emotional support canine for her.

"Is Buzz special?" Colton asked, staring at the husky.

Sarah looked at the dog again. "I mean, he's special in the sense that he's a great dog. But he's not of a championship bloodline or anything."

"That's strange that the man would say that then." Colton reached over and rubbed Buzz's head also. "Whoever killed Loretta must think you have something—something worth killing for."

Sarah wrapped her arms over her chest. "I agree. But it doesn't make sense. What am I going to do, Colton?"

Colton stood. "You should take that shower. Maybe it will help you clear your head."

She rose to her feet. "You're right. I need to get this blood off me."

Loretta's blood.

Nausea churned in her stomach.

Everything still felt surreal, like a nightmare.

Only Sarah knew she wouldn't wake up and everything wouldn't be better this time.

Colton waited until he heard the door to the bathroom open and close before he peered around the hallway.

Sarah's clothes were on the floor, neatly folded, just as he'd asked.

His heart twisted as he quietly stepped from his room, carefully picked the dress up and slipped it into a bag.

The clothing would most likely be needed as evidence. Though Sarah didn't want to tell the police what had happened, Colton hoped to make her come around. And, when she did, these clothes would need to be examined.

Though Sarah wanted to stay far away from the police, they would only help her. That was their job—to find the truth. Colton had no idea why her boss had told her not to talk to them. Was there more to that story? Or had the woman been delirious during her final moments?

Colton left the bag on the washing machine for the time being and then went into his bedroom. He opened the door to the attic and stepped inside, a musky smell enveloping him. He searched for a moment before finding what he wanted.

An old burgundy trunk. With a touch of trepidation, Colton opened the lid.

Sarah's old clothes stared back at him.

She'd left them at his old place when they thought they were getting married. She'd needed somewhere to store a few things, and his place had seemed like a logical choice. When he'd moved, he'd thought about getting rid of them. Why hadn't he?

He wasn't sure. It didn't matter now.

He rummaged through several things before pulling out some choices for Sarah.

Colton deposited the clothes for Sarah outside the bathroom door. He could still hear the water running on the other side and steam seeped from beneath the doorway.

He pulled out his phone, remembering that call he'd promised to make to find out more information on Loretta's death. He glanced at his watch. It was early—too early to make any inquiries without bringing attention to himself, which was the last thing Sarah would want.

But there was one person Colton could call. Fred Higgins. The man was his closest neighbor and one of the most vigilant people he knew. If there was any suspicious activity in this area, Fred would know about it.

The man always woke at the crack of dawn, and it was already past 7:00 a.m. Quickly, Colton dialed his number and waited for an answer. Mr. Higgins didn't disappoint.

"What I can I do for you, Hawk?"

"Morning, Higgins. Listen, did you hear anyone coming down our road last night?" Colton got right to the heart of the matter, knowing the ex-military man would appreciate his directness.

"Funny you ask that. As a matter of fact, I did. An old beat up sedan came through about four thirty, taking it real slow."

Sarah. That had to be Sarah's car. "An old friend is here visiting me."

"Good to know. Strange thing is that a few minutes later, another car crept by."

Colton's spine stiffened. "Is that right?"

Colton walked to the window and peered out, looking for any sign that someone was there. The sun hadn't risen yet, and everything was still clothed in darkness, making it nearly impossible to see.

"That's right. But it turned around and left a few minutes later. Figured someone got lost."

Colton wished he felt as confident about that. But at least he knew more now. "Thanks, Mr. Higgins."

"Everything okay?"

"It's fine. I know you like to keep an eye on this mountain. My friend thought she saw someone behind her."

"Well, she was right. But, like I said, that other car turned around."

But that also meant that someone knew where Sarah was. Most likely, the killer. The thought made Colton's stomach churn.

"Will you let me know if you see anyone else?" Colton asked.

"Absolutely."

Colton ended the call and leaned against the wall as the impact of this early morning's encounter hit him. Sarah... he never thought he'd see her again, especially not like this.

The two had met when he'd been a detective in Seattle. Sarah had worked in a coffee shop he liked to frequent. They started talking about some of the artwork hanging on the walls, and Sarah had finally admitted the paintings were hers and that she'd been working as a barista just until she got her big break in the art world.

After a month of coming in every day for coffee, Colton had finally asked her out. They were inseparable after that first date. They'd gotten engaged six months later and planned for a spring wedding.

But one night on a case, Colton had been forced to shoot an intoxicated, belligerent man who'd put innocent people in the line of fire. Guilt had haunted Colton ever since—especially when he remembered the rage the man's wife had toward him afterward. He wasn't a hero to her. No, he was the villain.

It wasn't long after that that Colton had decided to move from Seattle to northern Idaho. He wanted a slower pace of life in a more peaceful area. He wanted a lot of land and clean air and fewer demands.

Sarah had seemed onboard at first...and then she'd taken that job at an art gallery in Spokane, saying it was too big of an opportunity to pass up.

Apparently, that opportunity was bigger and more important than he was. His stomach clenched at the memories.

His life looked so much different today than it had two years ago. Colton had taken a break from police work. Instead, he built live-edge tables out in his barn.

His friend with the state police called him every month, asking when he wanted to come work for him. But Colton had refused. He'd know when the time was right to go back—if he ever did go back.

Despite all of that, sometimes he wished he could turn back time and go back to those days when his life had seemed so full. Back when he'd had someone to share his sorrows and joys. When his dreams of having a family had seemed close enough to touch.

There was no use dwelling on all of that now. He had other more pressing concerns to think about. The first thing he wanted to do right now was move Sarah's car out of sight—just in case.

He grabbed Sarah's car keys—she'd left them on the table—and then went outside and climbed into her sedan.

Colton cranked the engine and slowly pulled around to the back of his cabin.

As he did, he glanced around. This car was old. It was the one Sarah had back when they'd been engaged. And it had been unreliable then.

In fact, Colton was surprised the vehicle had even made it this far. It was probably fifteen years old, one of the seats was ripped and the engine made a puttering sound.

Colton put the car into Park and shook his head. Just what had happened with Sarah in the past two years?

His jaw tightened. It wasn't important. That wasn't his business. Nor was what kind of car Sarah was driving or what kind of condition it was in.

As he took the keys out of the ignition, he glanced on

the floor and saw a bag there. It seemed out of place in the vehicle. The leather looked expensive and new.

Colton started to reach for it and then stopped himself.

No, he wouldn't look inside. That was too intrusive. But his curiosity was sparked.

He glanced down at it one more time and saw a tag on the side labeling the bag as Buzz's. This must be dog supplies.

At that thought, he unzipped it, checking to see if there were items inside that he needed to take into his house for Buzz.

Instead, he saw money.

A lot of money.

Carefully, he prodded the bag open more. His eyes widened.

Just by looking, Colton would guess there was at least fifty thousand dollars there.

Where had Sarah gotten that money? He couldn't even begin to imagine.

Had she gotten in with the wrong crowd? Had she done something illegal?

Colton didn't like the conclusions that his mind started to form.

But he needed to be more cautious now than ever.

FOUR

Colton climbed out of Sarah's car, locked the doors and went back inside the house. He wandered into the kitchen and pulled out what food he had in his refrigerator. Maybe something to eat would help them sort out the situation.

He put some water on to boil for rice and found a can of gravy. This would work as dog food until he could get something else.

A few minutes later, Colton heard the water stop and the bathroom door open. The clothes disappeared from the hallway.

Colton's pulse pounded at the thought of talking to Sarah again. It had been so long, and there was so much he wanted to say to her, to ask her. But he needed to keep himself in check. The last thing he wanted was to get hurt again.

Buzz lay at his feet, keeping a watchful eye on the house. "Long night, huh, buddy?"

The dog stared back at him, seeming to take everything in.

"Your food is almost ready," Colton continued. "Maybe you could use something in your stomach too."

Buzz raised his nose to the air and sniffed his approval.

Just then, Sarah emerged from the hallway, her hair

wet and her skin flushed. Yet she looked adorable. She always did.

"Thank you for the clothes… I can't believe you kept them." She stopped at the kitchen counter, looking a touch self-conscious.

"I meant to get rid of them. I guess it's a good thing I didn't."

"I guess so."

Colton nodded toward the kitchen table. "Look, why don't you sit down? I'll fix some breakfast."

Her lips twisted down in an adorable half frown that Colton often thought about. It wasn't just that expression. He often thought about Sarah. He thought about her too much, for that matter.

He knew he needed to move on—to find someone who'd be more committed to him than a career. But there was no one else like Sarah. Despite that, she was off-limits.

"If you don't mind, then that sounds good. Thank you." She glanced around. "This place looks really great, by the way. It's rustic, but it's got a bit of style to it. Did you make this live-edge table yourself?"

He nodded and began scrambling some eggs in a bowl. "As a matter of fact, I did."

He liked working with his hands. It was quiet work that helped him to sort out his thoughts. He had a barn out back that he used as a workshop. He'd thought on more than one occasion about how much Sarah would enjoy a space like that to paint. The view of the mountains out the back was amazing.

As he poured the eggs into a sizzling pan, the timer went off. The rice was ready. He put the food in a bowl and waited for it to cool.

Buzz scooted a little closer, and Colton smiled, tossing down a small piece of egg for the dog to eat. A few minutes later, the omelets were finished, and Colton set the plates on the table so they could eat.

"Green onions, cheese and ham," he said. "Is that still good?"

He was rewarded with a smile.

"It's perfect," Sarah said. "Thank you."

He placed a bowl of rice and gravy on the floor for Buzz and then sat down. "So, how did you meet this Loretta woman?"

Sarah forced herself to swallow a bite of her breakfast, not hungry but trying to eat anyway. "It's kind of a strange story. I was actually participating in an art show in Spokane. It was outdoors. I saw Buzz near my booth. He'd stepped on something. I went over to help him and found a rock had gotten lodged in his paw."

"Poor guy."

Sarah flashed a bittersweet smile at the dog. "Yeah, he wasn't feeling too great. I decided to wait with him until his owner came back. Loretta showed up. Apparently, Buzz had gotten away from her. She was in her wheelchair and had attempted to take him out to the show. She offered me some money for my trouble. I told her I couldn't accept anything. She ended up coming over to my booth and purchasing a painting instead. She talked to me a little about my work, and genuinely seemed to like it."

"How did that lead to a job?"

Sarah put her fork down. "At that point, she knew my name and even my number—I'd given her my business card. She called me two months later and offered me a job as Buzz's caretaker, as well as part-time personal assistant. She said the job would still allow me time to work on my art. It was like an answer to prayer."

"It sounds like it."

"It wasn't always easy. Not at all. Loretta wasn't the

easiest to get along with. But I really respected the work she was doing in the medical community, and it was an honor to work for her. She was a medical researcher, and she developed a drug to help people with arthritis."

"That's great, Sarah."

She picked up her fork again but looked uncertain. "I know this sounds weird, but could we turn on the TV? I want to see if they're reporting Loretta's death yet and what they're saying about it if they are."

"Of course."

Colton flipped on the morning news. Breaking news aired over the station.

All the blood drained from Colton's face when Sarah's picture appeared on the screen. The headline proclaimed that Sarah Peterson, twenty-seven, was wanted for the murder of famed medical researcher Loretta Blanchard. The news anchor continued, saying that there was now a manhunt to find Sarah and warning viewers that she could be dangerous.

Sarah exchanged a look with Colton.

This was much, much worse than he'd imagined it would be.

Because not only was a killer potentially looking for Sarah, but so were the police.

"The police think I killed Loretta," Sarah murmured, her head spinning. "Why would they think that? I would never hurt anyone."

"Someone could have seen you run from the scene," Colton told her. "It would be a natural assumption."

She put her fork down, her thoughts clashing inside her until her head pounded. "You're right. Of course I look guilty. I was the last person seen with her. Her blood was on my sweater."

Colton squeezed her arm. "Don't panic yet. We could talk to the police, explain what happened—"

"I told you, no police. I can't risk it." Especially now that Sarah knew they thought she was guilty.

"The police aren't your enemy, Sarah." Colton's voice was quiet and calm—but also full of conviction.

"I didn't say they were. But Loretta had reasons for everything. There was a reason she said that. She…she was one of the smartest women I've ever met."

Colton frowned, looking as if he was trying to find the right words. "Not coming forward will only make you look more guilty."

Sarah shrugged, knowing his words were true but unable to verbally agree with him. "I just don't know what to say or do."

Colton opened his mouth, like he was about to say more. Before he could, his phone buzzed. He glanced at the screen and frowned again before answering.

Sarah tried to interpret the one-sided conversation but couldn't. She only knew something was wrong. Colton's voice sounded stiff, and he glanced at the window.

He ended the call and stood. "You and Buzz need to go to the back bedroom. Now. Lock the doors, and don't come out until I tell you."

Alarm raced through her. "Why? What's going on?"

"My neighbor saw someone coming up the lane toward the house." Colton walked toward the window.

"And that's strange?"

Colton looked back, locking gazes with her. "There are only two places they could be going—his house or mine, and neither of us are expecting anyone."

Sarah's heart rate surged. It was the killer, wasn't it? Or the police. Either way, her future looked bleak enough that nausea rose in her so quickly that she grasped her stomach.

"You need to go. Now." Colton pulled out the gun from his waistband, his jaw set with steely determination.

Sarah didn't argue. She scrambled away, hardly able to breathe.

But as she locked the door, Buzz beside her, she pressed her ear there, trying to hear what was going on.

It was silent as Colton waited, seeming to prepare himself for battle.

"Buzz, what's going on?" She reached down and wrapped her arms around the dog, relishing his soft fur.

The dog let out a whine and licked her cheek. Buzz knew something was wrong also.

Sarah waited, praying for safety and favor. But the moments felt like hours.

Flashbacks from earlier hit her, each one making her flinch. Images of seeing that man in Loretta's room. Watching as Loretta took her last breath.

Sarah remembered running. Fearing the man was following her. Fearing what he would do if he caught Sarah too.

Now Colton was in danger.

She stood and pressed herself into the wall, resisting the urge to look out the window and see what was going on.

She didn't have to.

She heard tires crunching on gravel in the distance.

Someone was here.

Sarah braced herself for whatever would happen next.

Colton rushed to the window, reaching for the gun at his waistband. Who would be coming here at this time of the day?

No one—unless it was an emergency or unless it was trouble.

His breath caught when no vehicles emerged at the end of the lane.

Someone had started this way and stopped.

Colton's instincts were finely tuned from years of law enforcement—finely tuned enough not to believe in coincidences, especially given the circumstances right now.

No. Someone had scoped out this place. Seen his cabin. And then returned.

That person was most likely the one who'd sent Sarah that threatening text.

He wanted whatever it was he thought Sarah had.

Colton couldn't let that happen. He *wouldn't* let that happen.

Without thinking about it anymore, Colton stepped outside. He glanced around, listening for any signs of trouble.

He heard nothing.

Cautiously, he walked down his road, his gun still in hand.

He was never one to cower away from trouble, and he wasn't going to start now.

With every step, Colton listened for any clues that someone was near. Stalking. Waiting.

He anticipated hearing footsteps. Twigs cracking.

All was silent except for the occasional rustle of wind or the crackle of icy snow beneath his boots.

He still didn't let down his guard. If this criminal was in any way trained, he would know to disguise his presence. And based on everything Sarah had told him, this man very well could be someone who hadn't killed in the heat of the moment but in premeditated murder. The thought wasn't comforting.

As Colton turned the corner, he spotted a dark sedan tucked away at the end of the lane.

He froze. His heart pounded in his ears as anticipation built inside him. What was the driver doing?

The car didn't move, and the windows were too tinted

to see inside. The driver could be there…or he could have slipped out.

Colton's gaze traveled to the front of the car, but the license plate was concealed by the brush.

Quickly, he scanned the woods.

Was the driver waiting behind one of these trees, watching Colton's every move?

Colton heard nothing around him.

Cautiously, he took another step.

He wasn't leaving here until he knew who was inside that car or until he at least got a license plate.

With every step, he listened, keenly aware of everything around him.

Suddenly, the car's engine revved.

A moment later, the car charged toward him.

FIVE

What was taking so long? What was Colton doing out there? Sarah wondered.

A few minutes ago, it had sounded like the front door opened. Had Colton gone outside?

What if he was hurt right now? Hurt because Sarah had brought danger into his quiet life, the life that was supposed to keep him from situations like this one.

She glanced down at Buzz. The dog stared at her, as if trying to communicate, before letting out a bark.

"Something's wrong, isn't it?" she murmured.

Buzz barked again.

Sarah shushed him, trying not to draw any more attention to them than necessary. Buzz's barking could alert an intruder that they were here. Since she had no idea what was going on outside this room, she had to be cautious.

Taking a tentative step, Sarah went to the window and peered out. Just as she shoved the curtain aside, she saw a car careen toward Colton at the end of the lane.

She braced herself for whatever would happen next while frantically praying.

Please, Lord, help him. Keep him safe. Please!

Just before the car hit him, Colton dove into the woods.

The black sedan did a swift U-turn. Then it sped off, leaving a trail of dust behind it.

Was Colton okay?

Sarah couldn't stay in here any longer. She had to check on him.

If he got hurt because of her, then she'd never forgive herself.

"Come on, Buzz," she called.

The dog remained on Sarah's heels as she ran outside. Her bare feet crunched in the thick snow, and a painful ache began because of the cold. Her wet hair slapped her face before the strands froze together in clumps. Icy air invaded her lungs.

She didn't care.

Colton could be in danger right now.

Moving as quickly as she could, Sarah hit the gravel road. Her feet were already numb now as they hit the rocky soil.

All she could think about was Colton and whether or not he was okay. That driver had tried to run him down.

The seriousness of the situation hit her again. Whoever was behind all of this wasn't playing games. He'd rather kill again than risk being exposed.

Sarah pushed down a sliver of fear.

Just as she reached the end of the lane, Colton emerged from the woods. He rubbed his head and his eyes were narrow with irritation, but he otherwise looked okay.

Thank goodness.

She rushed toward him, stopping just short of touching him. She paused there, a bone-chilling wind sweeping around her, sending clumps of snow from the branches above down on them.

"Sarah, you shouldn't be out here."

"Are you okay?" she asked, still worried about him

and studying his features for any sign that something was wrong. "I couldn't leave you."

"I'm okay. But I don't want that man to see you if he comes back." He took her elbow and turned her around. "Come on. Let's get inside. Besides, you're going to freeze out here."

She ignored the charge of electricity she felt rush through her at his touch.

This was no time for electricity. Besides, she and Colton were finished. Done. There was no going back to fix what had happened between them.

Colton might forgive, but he didn't forget.

Not that Sarah would ever want to get back together with him. It didn't matter that she'd missed him and his companionship. Missed the kisses they'd shared. Missed the possibility of spending the future with someone.

But everyone she'd ever loved had disappointed her. Why should Colton be different?

Sarah had so many questions she wanted to ask about what had just happened. But she held them in.

For now.

Instead, she listened for a minute. She didn't hear the car. Didn't hear footsteps or yells. Buzz seemed calm.

Those were all good things, but she didn't know how long they would last.

As soon as they stepped into his cabin, Colton locked the door and then peered out the window again. His entire body looked tense and on alert.

"Is the man still there?" Sarah demanded, a surge of anxiety rising in her. What if he came back? What if he killed all of them, just like he'd killed Loretta?

Colton's gaze remained focused out the window. "I don't see him. Was that the car that followed you?"

"I… I don't know. Maybe. It was so dark that I could

really only see headlights. But whoever was driving the car just now left. What does that mean? If he knew I was here, wouldn't he have stayed?" Sarah walked toward the fire, unable to ignore just how cold she was and how badly her feet hurt.

"He may have been feeling this area out. If he lost you as you came down the road, then he may have come here looking for your car. He may be looking for confirmation."

"My car…" Sarah's heart skipped a beat. It had been out front, hadn't it? She hadn't been paying attention, but that was where she left it.

Colton looked back at her, his gaze softening. "I moved it behind the house, so he didn't see it. I don't think he saw you when you ran out either."

"He could have killed you." The words caught in Sarah's throat. No matter what had happened between the two of them in the past, she couldn't live with herself if something happened to Colton because of her.

"He could have. But, most likely, he doesn't know with certainty that I know you. If he knew you were here, he would have kept on going right to the house to find you and complete his mission."

"You think?" She shuddered. That had been close. So, so close.

"He was aggressive. He wouldn't have let me stop him."

"Maybe he'll move on now…" Sarah walked over to the window and glanced out also, half expecting to see the car again.

Instead, the peaceful woods stared back, the early morning sky stretching above the frosted evergreens.

Colton's expression remained grim, as if he didn't want to give her false hope. "If he suspects you're in this area, then he'll keep on looking."

Sarah trembled again. "So what should I do?"

His jaw tightened with resolve as he continued to stare out the window, not saying anything for a minute. "We don't have any choice but to get out of here. We have to operate as if this is a worst-case scenario. That guy could come back—we don't want to be here if he does."

"We?" The words came out as a squeak, and Sarah's hand flew to her throat.

Colton nodded. "I can't send you out there alone, Sarah."

"I… I don't want to put you at risk." She'd pulled him into danger with her. What had she been thinking? Why had she come here? She would have been better off driving until her car couldn't make it any farther.

But when she'd thought of safety, Colton was the first person who had come to mind.

Colton stepped closer and lowered his voice. "You're not. I'm going with you, Sarah. Nothing you say will change my mind."

She didn't want to feel pleased. Didn't want to feel the shiver that rushed down her spine. Didn't want to find benefit in the thought that someone else was in harm's way.

But Sarah did feel relief wash through her.

Because she knew she couldn't do this on her own. And Sarah *could* do it with Colton by her side. But their history was going to be their biggest obstacle.

Colton's eyes continually scanned the road as he traveled from his cabin into the majestic countryside. Snowcapped peaks surrounded him, along with rocky terrain and what in the summer months was a rollicking river.

These were the things he'd moved to the area for—the peace and serenity of wide-open spaces and clean air.

But right now, he found no joy in his surroundings. Not knowing what he did. Not with everything he'd learned that was going on with Sarah.

He hadn't seen the dark-colored sedan since he'd left his cabin twenty minutes ago, but he still didn't let down his guard. Someone who was determined to kill Sarah wouldn't give up that easily.

They'd left quickly. Sarah had packed up some of her old clothes, as well as a few extra supplies for Buzz, including a water dish. Colton had also packed a bag, as well as some snacks and water. He'd slipped Sarah's bloody clothing into the bottom of his duffel, just in case. He didn't want to leave them there for just anyone to discover.

Glancing in the backseat, he also saw that Sarah had grabbed the bag from her car. She didn't act suspicious, like she felt guilty about whatever was inside.

But Colton couldn't stop thinking about it. Maybe Sarah had sold a painting. Maybe she had a good explanation for having that kind of cash.

But what if she didn't?

He would ask her. Soon. When the time was right.

"Where are we going?" Sarah's arm snaked into the backseat of his double cab, and she rubbed Buzz's head. She'd done that often since they left, and the dog's presence seemed to calm her.

She wore some old jeans and a blue flannel shirt. Her hair—wet when they'd left—had been pulled back into a bun. She had no makeup on, but she didn't need any. Her skin looked perfect just the way it was. Colton had given her an old jacket of his—a thick black one that would keep her warm outside. She'd also found some old boots in that trunk, back from when they used to go hiking together.

Colton glanced at Buzz again. He liked having the dog with them. The canine had perceptive eyes, and he always stood on guard. Without ever witnessing it, he could tell that Buzz would do whatever it took to protect Sarah.

"I think we should go back to Spokane," he told Sarah.

Sarah's wide eyes focused on him. "Spokane? Why would we go back there? Shouldn't we get as far away as possible?"

"A couple of reasons. First of all, I doubt this guy would think you'd go back."

"That could be true, I guess." She shrugged, still looking uncertain.

"Second, I think we need to figure out what happened to Loretta ourselves."

"Why would we do that?" Sarah's voice climbed with anxiety. "I mean, the police are looking for me. Won't they be more likely to find me there in Spokane?"

"I realize that, so we'll need to be careful. But I think the only way we're going to put this behind us is to find answers ourselves."

She gasped and paused before she said, "You think we should find the killer? Is that what you're saying."

"Yeah, I guess that's what I'm saying." Colton knew it sounded crazy, but he'd worked in law enforcement for more than a decade. If he trusted his instincts, he knew this was the right plan.

"How are we going to do that?"

Colton stared straight ahead as the sun peeked just over the trees, the new day settling in for a while. "We need to talk. I need more information."

"I can do that but…what about your work? I know you have a job. You can't just leave." Sarah sounded halfway panicked and halfway guilt ridden.

It was kind of her to be concerned about him. Sarah had always been sensitive and intuitive. It made her a great artist. She picked up on things that others didn't.

At one time, Colton had loved that about her.

"I'm just doing some woodworking right now, Sarah. I'm on sabbatical from my work in law enforcement."

"But—"

He glanced at her and shook his head, trying to nip this conversation in the bud. "No buts about it. Now, tell me more about your boss."

Sarah shifted, pulling her arm back into her lap and staring straight ahead at the road. "Loretta? I hardly know what to say. She was…she was esteemed in the medical community. She was a real genius."

"Did she have enemies?"

"I… I don't know. I mean, I didn't work for her that long, so I didn't get to meet many people who knew her. She was demanding and a perfectionist. I guess that's why she was good at her job. But she also had ALS. She was in a wheelchair. She didn't even have a chance to defend herself…" Sarah's voice broke as tears streamed down her face.

"I'm sorry, Sarah." Colton's heart squeezed with compassion. This situation would be a lot for anyone, but for someone as tenderhearted as Sarah it would be devastating.

"I just keep picturing her. I keep seeing her in her room, on the floor, with the man standing over her. It was so horrible, Colton." She sniffled again and used her sleeve to wipe beneath her eyes.

He reached over and squeezed her knee. Colton hadn't intended on touching Sarah, but he couldn't stand to see her looking so alone, especially considering what she'd been through. No one should have to be so isolated in their suffering—not when they had someone right beside them.

"Seeing that would be hard on anyone," he murmured.

Using her sleeve, Sarah wiped beneath her eyes again. "I've always known that there's danger in the world. But seeing it firsthand… I just can't stop thinking about it."

"We're going to get through this, Sarah." There Colton went again, promising Sarah things. Promising a future—

no matter how potentially long or short. Their paths were intertwined, for now, at least.

Just as he said the words, a black sedan came into view behind him.

Colton pulled his hand back from Sarah's knee and gripped the steering wheel, his law enforcement training kicking into gear.

"What is it?" Sarah asked, glancing behind them. "Is that the car?"

"I don't know. But I'm not taking any chances."

SIX

Sarah gripped the door handle, her lungs frozen as she waited to see what would happen next. Would the driver try to run them of the road? Would he shoot? Try to kill them?

She had no idea. But each possibility made her head pound harder.

How had her life turned into such a nightmare? Things had just seemed to be getting back on track. She finally found a better place to live. Another job. All her mistakes seemed to be haunting her less and less.

And now this?

She glanced over her shoulder again. The sedan was still back there, but it wasn't close. No, the driver kept a decent distance behind them.

Maybe that was a good sign, an indication they'd be safe for a while longer. But Sarah knew the interlude wouldn't last for long. If Sarah had to guess, they were still forty-five minutes away from Spokane. The town was almost two hours from Colton's house, which was just north of Coeur d'Alene, Idaho.

Expertly, Colton began weaving in and out of traffic. The closer they came to Spokane, the more congestion they'd encountered. It was mostly commuters, some logging trucks and a few semis.

"What are we going to do?" Sarah couldn't seem to stop asking that question.

"We're going to lose them." Colton sounded so confident as he said the words. He always had that calm, soothing way about him. While everyone else panicked, he calmly assessed a situation and became the hero.

She gripped the door harder as her thoughts continued to race. "How did he even find us again? He wasn't back there when we left. I've been watching, and I know you have also."

Colton glanced in the rearview mirror. "He must be tracking you somehow. It's the only thing that makes sense."

"How in the world would he track me?"

"I only have one guess. Your phone."

"My phone…?" It made sense, Sarah supposed. The man had her number—he'd called her using Loretta's cell. The device had a GPS locater that he could have somehow tapped into, if he had the right skills or knowledge. "What should I do? Throw it out the window?"

"No, I have another idea. I don't think he knows for sure that we're in this truck." He eased into another lane.

"Why do you say that?"

Colton glanced in the rearview mirror again and pressed the accelerator harder. "It's just a hunch. He seems to be keeping his options open and staying behind several vehicles. I'm going to play a little game with him so I can know for sure."

Sarah nodded, her throat tight. She was going to have to trust Colton on this one because she had other ideas about what they should be doing.

As the road curved up ahead, Colton hit the accelerator and sped just out of sight. He turned at a large gas station and parked beside a semitruck. Moving quickly, he took Sarah's phone, instructed her to stay in the car, and then rushed out.

As Colton walked past the back of the semitruck, he nestled the phone in the back bumper of the vehicle. Based on the snug fit, it should stay there for a while.

He glanced around.

No one looked his way.

Moving quickly, Colton headed back to his car, jumped into the driver's seat and sped around to the back of the building to wait.

"Why are we staying here?" Sarah's voice sounded breathless with fear.

"I need to see what happens." The semi was just in his line of sight. He had to keep a careful eye on it. Otherwise, his plan would be all for nothing.

"If your guess is wrong, then we're sitting ducks," Sarah whispered.

Her words were a somber reminder. She was right. The stakes were high right now—it could cost them their lives. But he had to rely on his gut instinct at the moment. It was all he had.

"You're right," Colton said. "So let's hope I'm not wrong."

"Comforting." Sarah crossed her arms and slunk down lower.

Though Colton was just out of sight, he could still see the truck where he'd planted Sarah's phone. He watched carefully, waiting for the black sedan to appear.

His breath caught when he saw the car slowly creep into the parking lot and pull into a space.

Part of Colton wanted to get out and confront the driver right here. But he couldn't do that. The man could be dangerous—could have a gun and put other people at risk. No, Colton had other ideas right now—ideas that required patience.

"Colton?"

He raised a finger, asking for silence. "Just a minute."

He could feel the tension—the fear—in the car. Even Buzz seemed to notice. The dog stuck his nose into the front seat and sniffled, like he smelled danger was near.

A minute later, the semitrailer pulled out of the lot. Colton waited, watching to see what would happen next.

The sedan pulled out after it.

Sarah gasped. "Wait…"

"Someone *was* tracking the phone."

After giving the driver a good head start, Colton followed as he headed down the road. He wanted to follow this car. See who was inside.

Because the driver had some answers—answers they needed.

But there was also more than one way to figure out who was behind that wheel.

With his eyes on the car, he pulled out his phone and called a friend, Jim Larsen, with the highway patrol.

"Colton, what can I do for you?"

"Hey, Jim. I need you to run some plates for me for a case I'm working," Colton said. "Would you mind?"

"Not at all. What do you have?"

Colton rattled off the license plate.

"I'll do it right now. One second."

Colton waited, anxious to hear what Jim found out.

A moment later, his friend came back on the line. "Car belongs to a Randolph Stephens in Spokane."

"Randolph Stephens?" Colton repeated, glancing at Sarah.

She shrugged, indicating the name wasn't familiar.

"Anything else on this guy?" Colton asked.

"I don't see any priors. Not even a parking ticket."

"That's great. Thank you, Jim."

Colton ended the call. At least it was something. He'd take whatever information he could get right now.

Randolph Stephens?

Sarah turned the name over in her head as they continued down the highway.

Had Loretta ever said the name?

Sarah didn't think so. She'd probably remember a name like Randolph. It was unique enough that she didn't hear it often.

Colton handed her his phone. "Do me a favor. Do an internet search for me for this Randolph Stephens guy. Tell me if anything comes up or if he looks familiar."

Sarah took the device from him and stared at the screen a moment. "I need your code."

Colton swallowed so hard that his neck muscles pulled taut. "It's 0521."

"0521?"

"Yes," he confirmed.

That was supposed to be their wedding date. Sarah kept the thought to herself, not wanting to make this situation any more awkward than it had to be.

"I never got around to changing it," Colton muttered, his jaw muscle jumping.

"I get it." It was nothing, Sarah told herself. No, like Colton said, he'd just gotten comfortable with the numbers and left them. That news didn't mean that he still cared about Sarah or that he still felt any heartbreak over their split.

Pushing aside her thoughts, Sarah typed in the name.

Only one person with the name Randolph Stephens popped up in Spokane. Sarah stared at the man's picture, hoping for a light bulb moment. But there was nothing. The dark-haired man with a receding hairline was unfamiliar to her.

"Here it is," Sarah told Colton. "Randolph is fifty-two years old, and he's an engineer. He volunteers for numerous organizations. Has a wife, three children and one grandchild, it looks like, according to his social media. This guy doesn't look like a killer."

"That doesn't mean anything. Is there any resemblance to the man you saw at Loretta's?"

Sarah shook her head. "In this picture, Randolph's wife looks taller than he is. The man I saw was big and burly. Not like this."

Colton frowned. "I see."

"But according to that state trooper you called, that car belonged to Randolph…"

"We'll have to look into it more a little later." Colton wove around some cars, trying to keep the sedan in sight.

"What?" Colton muttered, his gaze flickering to the right.

"What's wrong?" Sarah asked.

"He just turned off the highway," Colton muttered.

He accelerated back into the right lane, trying to get over before he missed the exit. The cars behind him laid on their horns. Colton wasn't swayed. He continued to follow the man who had once been following them.

Just then, another logging truck pulled in front of them. Sarah gasped as Colton pressed on the brakes and leaned to the side, trying to see around the truck.

"Is he still in eyesight?" Sarah asked.

Colton's jaw tightened. "It's no use. The whole lane is now blocked."

"You can't get around?" As Sarah asked the question, she glanced beside them. The road had a sharp drop-off.

There was no wiggle room to ease onto the shoulder.

And the logging truck had slowed as the road became an incline. As Colton slowed also, Sarah knew that they were losing the sedan.

Finally, they reached the top of the hill, and the road opened up again. Colton pulled his car into the left lane to pass the other vehicles.

But the sedan was gone.

Colton hit his hand against the steering wheel.

"We lost him," he muttered. "The driver either got off this road, or he's so far ahead that we won't be able to catch him."

"I'm sorry, Colton." Disappointment spread through Sarah. They'd been close. So close.

"The good news is that he also lost us."

"So we're safe?"

Colton frowned. "For a minute."

Sarah glanced at Colton and studied his expression— the set of his eyes and jaw. "But you don't think this is over, do you?"

He turned to her. "I think this is a long way from being over."

SEVEN

Colton's jaw tightened as he stared straight ahead at the road. He couldn't believe he'd lost the sedan. If only that logging truck hadn't cut in front of him. If only the road hadn't narrowed. If only the incline hadn't been so steep. But it had been.

And somehow the driver—along with their best lead for finding answers—had gotten away.

Sarah cleared her throat beside him. "Did you ever call any of your police contacts and see if you could find out anything about what happened? I know it's asking a lot but—"

"No, I haven't made any calls yet. But I will. Now." He had nothing to do but drive, and the sooner they had answers, the better.

"And, I hate to bring it up, but I'm going to need a restroom break before too long. Could we stop somewhere?"

"Yes, let's do that." Colton had planned on doing it sometime, but now, as they were getting closer to town, seemed like just as good a time as any.

He pulled up to a convenience store, a larger one that sold various items, and paused. "How about you go in alone, and I'll wait out here, keeping an eye out? Maybe I'll let Buzz stretch his legs also."

"That sounds good." She grabbed her purse. "I won't be long."

He watched as Sarah went into the store. There were several cars in the lot, so she wouldn't be the only person inside. Hopefully, no one would recognize her. Either way, Colton felt like he would serve her better by remaining lookout near the door.

It would also give him the chance to call one of his contacts and to speak freely.

He stepped out of the truck, Buzz's leash in hand, and wandered to a grassy area to the side of the building. As Buzz sniffed around, Colton dialed the number for Detective Ben Simmons, one of his contacts in Spokane. He'd worked with Simmons back in Seattle, and the two had a good relationship.

"Hello?" his friend's voice rang through the line.

"Hey, man. It's Colton."

After a couple minutes of chitchat, Colton swallowed hard. "Listen, I have two questions."

"Shoot."

"First, I was hoping you could do some research for me on a man named Randolph Stephens. He's from the Spokane area."

"What do you need to know?"

"Could you see if he's reported any vehicles that have been stolen?" Colton's gut told him that was what had happened, but he needed confirmation.

"Sure thing. What else?"

Colton shifted, entirely more uncomfortable with his next question. "I was watching the news, and I saw a story about that medical researcher who was killed in the area."

"Loretta Blanchard. Yes, it's a huge loss for our community. The woman was brilliant and respected."

"That is quite the loss," Colton said, watching as another car pulled into the lot. A woman with a young son scrambled toward the door. Still no signs of trouble. Good. "But I also heard that someone named Sarah Peterson was a person of interest."

"That's right. You sound like you know something…"

Colton shifted, still scanning everything around them. "I was actually engaged to Sarah. She couldn't have done this."

As he said the words, he knew they were true. Sarah was many things—but she wasn't a killer.

"How long ago did you say it had been since you were engaged?" Ben asked.

"Two years." Sometimes it seemed like just yesterday, and other times it seemed like another lifetime ago.

"Well, a lot could have changed in two years. Apparently, Ms. Peterson worked for Ms. Blanchard, but from everything I'm hearing, the two of them didn't really get along."

Colton sucked in a breath at the news. "Why do you say that?"

"That's the word from people who knew Loretta. Loretta was always fussing about her newest employee, saying she wasn't tidy enough. That she stayed out too late. That she got things done too slowly."

"Maybe Loretta was just a fussy type of person."

Ben let out a chuckle. "She was. I can assure you of that. But this woman—your ex-fiancée—comes on to the scene out of the blue and then Loretta was murdered. That in itself is suspicious."

"That doesn't mean she's guilty," Colton reminded him, the tension in his shoulders growing by the minute.

"Ms. Peterson's prints were found on the murder weapon."

"What murder weapon is that?"

"Some scissors. And about fifty thousand dollars of Loretta's money is gone. Loretta made a cash withdrawal earlier today, and it's no longer in her house. No one in her inner circle knows what she would have done with it."

He remembered the bag in Sarah's sedan. Could that have been…?

Colton shook his head. No. She wouldn't have done that. Sarah wasn't the type.

"The real killer could have taken it," Colton said.

"That's right. The real killer. And that may have been your ex-fiancée."

"There are a lot of assumptions here."

"We also found some of Loretta's jewelry in Ms. Peterson's room. We think she fled so quickly that she forgot to take it."

The killer had to have planted that jewelry. He was the one who'd taken that money. It was the only thing that made sense.

"Thanks for your help," Colton finally said.

"I appreciate you calling to offer your perspective. But your ex-fiancée is still our prime suspect."

"Good to know." He ended the call just as Sarah began walking back toward the truck.

He had some hard questions to ask her. He really hoped that the conclusion that wanted to form in his head was incorrect. Because he didn't want to think that Sarah had anything to do with Loretta's death…but the evidence was stacking up and becoming harder to ignore.

Sarah climbed back in the truck. As soon as she saw Colton's face, she sensed something was wrong.

He lowered his phone. What exactly had the phone call turned up? Whatever it was, it wasn't good.

"What happened?" she asked hurriedly. "Is something else wrong?"

Colton pressed his lips together, the same way he always did when he dreaded something. "Sarah, I have to ask you something, and I don't want to waste any words. Did you take money from Loretta?"

The blood drained from her face. "What? Colton—"

"I'm just asking." His eyes were level, as was his voice. He seriously wanted to know.

"You saw that threatening message," she reminded him. "You know I didn't do this."

His gaze locked on to hers. "Then why aren't you answering my question?"

"I did answer it."

"What was that bag in your car?"

"That bag in my car—" Sarah stopped short.

She'd grabbed Buzz's bag, only because it had been by the back door. She'd given it little thought since she'd taken it before leaving Loretta's house.

"What were you going to say, Sarah?" Colton asked her.

"Nothing of importance. I kept a backpack by the back door, and I always took it with me when I walked Buzz. I grabbed it on my way out."

"Have you looked inside?"

"Why would I? I haven't needed the treats or anything else. I've had other things on my mind."

"Look inside." Colton's words left no room for argument.

Sarah reached into the backseat of the truck, grabbed the bag and unzipped it. She gasped at what she saw inside. Reaching in, she pulled out a stack of one-hundred-dollar bills. "Where did this come from?"

"You didn't know it was there?"

"I had no idea. Why would Loretta put money in Buzz's bag, especially such a large amount?"

Colton stared at her.

Sarah's mouth gaped open as she realized what he wasn't saying. "What? You think I stole this and put it here?"

"I didn't say that. I'm just gathering information."

"Colton, you've got to believe me. I had no idea."

"Why *would* Loretta give you that much money? That much cash? There are thousands and thousands of dollars in there."

"I have no idea. To take care of Buzz, maybe? Buzz was her baby. She didn't have children, so the dog was her life."

"Is there anything you need to tell me?"

The pointedness of Colton's question caused a jolt of alarm to shoot through Sarah. "No, there's not. Why? What are you getting at?"

"Did you take some of your boss's jewelry?"

"No!" Her jewelry? Sarah sucked in a breath as she realized the truth. "I mean, yes. I mean—"

"What is it, Sarah?" Colton's tone made it clear he was losing patience with her and beginning to doubt her story.

"It's not like that. I did have some of her jewelry. I was supposed to take it in to be cleaned. It was actually on my agenda for today—back before everything went haywire. I had the appointment at Goodwind's Jewelry. You can call and ask them. I had an appointment set up and everything."

"I may have to do that." His voice held a sharp edge and he turned away from her. He put the truck into Reverse, backed out and took off again down the road.

Panic began to rise in her. Sarah started to reach for Colton, but she stopped herself and swallowed hard instead. She had to convince him she was telling the truth—because she was.

"Colton, I know how this looks. But I didn't want her money. I'm not that kind of person."

"But you were having trouble. With your job. With making ends meet."

Heat rushed to Sarah's cheeks at the starkness of his words. "But I wouldn't steal. You know me better than that. Do you really think I would do that?"

"It's been two years, Sarah. I have to ask these questions."

She shook her head and looked away, unwilling to let Colton see her tears. She didn't think it would hurt this much to have Colton doubt her, but it did. "It's been two years, but you still know who I am. You know my character. At least, I thought you did."

Colton touched her knee, jolting her. "I'm sorry, Sarah. I'd be foolish not to ask. I really don't know what's happened in the years since I've seen you. That's the truth. People change whether we want to admit it or not."

"It's like I told you—I moved to Spokane and got a job at that art gallery. I don't have much money, but what I do have is mine and no one else's. I earned it rightfully."

"But you're not there anymore, are you? Or are you working more than one job?"

"No, I'm not working at that gallery anymore."

"Instead you moved in with someone and took on the side job of being her personal assistant and a caretaker to her dog. What happened?"

She frowned. "Let's just say that my boss at the art gallery didn't exactly hire me because he respected my knowledge of the art world."

Colton's eyes widened. "Did he proposition you?"

"He made it clear that he hired me because he thought

I was nice to look at and that he hoped our relationship might grow into something more." Her stomach roiled as the words left her lips. "And, if it didn't, well… I couldn't expect my career to progress."

"What did you do?"

"I quit, of course." Her voice rose with outrage. "There was no way I could work for him anymore."

Colton's shoulders visibly relaxed. "It sounds like you made the right choice."

She nodded, heaviness pressing on her. "I know I did. But it was hard to find another job. John Abram—that was his name—called the other galleries in town and made up some lies about me."

"What kind of lies?"

"He said that I stole from him." She let out a bitter laugh and shook her head. "I know it sounds unbelievable that two people would say I'm guilty of stealing. But I didn't do it. At Loretta's or at John's. I was trying to do whatever I could to make ends meet and that's why I took a job working for Loretta."

"I'm sorry, Sarah." Colton's voice sounded soft and concerned.

She ignored the warm feelings that Colton's reaction brought—memories of better times. Of feeling loved and protected.

Those days were over, and she'd be wise to remember that.

"Life doesn't always turn out the way we expect, does it?" she murmured.

Colton shook his head. "No, it doesn't."

His words hung in the air, and neither was able to forget them.

Never in a million years would Sarah have thought she'd

be running for her life. That such simple life choices could have such disastrous effects.

But now her life was on the line—and so was Colton's. Deep down inside, she wasn't confident either of them were going to get out of this alive.

EIGHT

As Colton continued to head down the road, he couldn't stop thinking about what Sarah had told him.

All he'd ever wanted to do was take care of Sarah. Yet she'd pushed him away. Made up an excuse about being unable to pass up her job offer. Said she couldn't see herself living in the country and away from life as she knew it.

Colton's heart had been crushed. He'd tried to talk her into staying, but her mind had been made up. She'd given him the engagement ring back and said goodbye.

But she'd been crying as she'd driven away. Colton had seen the tears.

Colton couldn't—and didn't—try to make Sarah do anything she didn't want to do. If Sarah stayed with him, then he'd wanted it to be because she chose to do so.

She'd made her choice two years ago. Once she'd walked away, Colton was done. He wasn't going to beg someone who didn't want to be a part of his life to remain a part of it. Colton's heart had been broken; he knew there was no going back.

He wasn't the type who easily forgot the sting of rejection. Sarah had made her choice.

But, as hard as all of that was and as resolute as he felt

to stick with his convictions, he did want to be there for Sarah now.

Colton continued down the road, at once remembering how much he and Sarah had loved road trips together. On his time off, they'd taken trips to see the redwoods, to explore waterfalls, to marvel at mountains. She'd helped to open his eyes to the wonders around him and reminded him to take time to breathe.

Those times were behind him. A bittersweet memory.

Instead, he glanced at the road ahead. They were almost in Spokane now. Behind him, he could see the mountains where his home was nestled in his rearview mirror.

"So, what are we going to do when we get to Spokane?" Sarah asked, still looking shaken.

"I've been thinking about that. We're going to have to talk to some people who knew Loretta. We need to find out who her enemies were. It's the only way we'll get to the bottom of this."

"It makes sense."

He glanced at Sarah again, watching as the mountainside blurred past her window. "So, who did Loretta talk to? Did she go into an office? Did she have a circle of friends?"

Sarah wrapped her arms across her chest and frowned. "Loretta was a bit reclusive—at least, she was in the time I knew her. But…well, she worked in the office up until six months ago, from my understanding."

"What happened then?"

"Her health started to go downhill. She's had ALS for several years, but it took a turn for the worse recently. I think she was really struggling with the change and felt like she should be able to push through it. Finally, she realized she couldn't."

"Did she ever mention anyone from the lab?"

Sarah stared out the window and narrowed her eyes with thought. "There was one woman…her name was Debbie Wilcox. If I remember correctly, Debbie was the CFO of Loretta's company."

"Did you ever meet her?"

"No, I didn't. I only heard Loretta talking about her. Apparently, she was Loretta's right-hand woman. The two seemed close."

It was a starting place, at least. "What was the name of her company?"

"Blanchard Pharmaceuticals. Why?" Sarah turned toward him, her wide eyes searching his.

"I think we should start there. See what Debbie knows."

"What are you going to tell her? You're not officially on this case…"

Colton's jaw tightened as he thought through the legalities of everything. "I'll tell her that I'm investigating Loretta's death."

"What about me? When she sees me, she'll know the truth. My picture has been on the news." Sarah's voice cracked as she said the words.

"You're going to have to stay with Buzz. I don't like the idea of it, but we don't have any other choice. Yes, you are recognizable. But Buzz? Everyone's suspicions about you would be confirmed if they see him."

Sarah nodded and turned back toward the window. "I understand."

Sarah might understand, but Colton didn't like this situation any more than she did. But there was little he could do to change it at this point. No, they needed answers and they didn't have time to come up with a Plan B.

Sarah's life depended on Colton keeping her safe…and that was a task he didn't take lightly.

* * *

Apprehension continued to rise in Sarah as they drew closer to the Spokane area. What if someone here recognized her?

If the wrong person found her, she could be put away. For life.

It had happened to her mother. She'd been arrested for stealing money from her boss. She'd claimed she'd only done so in order to buy groceries, but prosecutors hadn't cared. She'd been given a five-year prison sentence, and Sarah and her sister had been put into foster care.

Sarah's mom had appealed. But, before anything could go through, she'd had a heart attack while in prison and died before ever seeing freedom again.

Sarah and her sister were forced to live alone in the system. Their dad had left when Sarah was six, and he hadn't reappeared in their lives.

Since all of that happened, trusting people hadn't come easily for Sarah.

When Colton had begun to pull away after a particularly heart-wrenching case, she'd seen the red flags. He'd never acknowledged the change in himself. No, he'd been in denial. But he'd become withdrawn. Aloof. He still said he loved her, but Sarah knew the truth: love could turn on a dime. What one minute seemed like happily-ever-after could fade into a nightmare.

So it had been better that Sarah had just left. Gone away to start a safe life without anyone to hurt her.

But the decision still haunted her every day. Every day Sarah wondered how life could have turned out differently. If Colton would have bounced back from his last case. If they'd be happy together now.

It didn't matter. Those times were behind her now.

Colton put his truck in Park in front of the six-story

building where Loretta worked. He reached into his glove compartment and pulled out a hat and sunglasses. "Put these on. Just in case anyone sees you."

A surge of panic rushed through Sarah. "What if the man in the sedan comes back…"

"He shouldn't have a way of tracking you right now. If you stay low, you should be okay." Colton thrust something into her hands. "But if someone approaches you, I want you to drive away."

"What about you?"

"I'll be fine."

"But—"

His gaze locked with hers. "No buts about it. If you see trouble, you leave. Understand?"

She nodded, though she felt anything but okay. His look didn't leave much room for argument. "How long will you be?"

"I have no idea, but I'll try to be quick." Colton lowered his voice. "We're going to figure this out."

He kept saying that. But Sarah had little hope that would happen. She knew how these things worked. She didn't have money to defend herself if the cops pressed charges.

She was going to end up like her mom. In jail until she died.

Her throat ached.

Instead of expressing those fears, she simply said, "Okay."

Colton stared at her one more moment before nodding. "I'll be back as soon as I can. Buzz, keep an eye on her for me, okay?"

Buzz nuzzled his hand in response.

Sarah watched as Colton disappeared inside the building. Then she slunk low in her seat and watched everyone around her. The office building was located in the downtown area so plenty of people were out and about, going to and from their office buildings.

No one seemed to be staring at them. Thank goodness.

She'd been to this area many times. Mostly there were offices but, just two blocks away, there were some restaurants. One block in the opposite direction there was a little park with some trails cut through small wooded areas, a playground and a breathtaking view of the river.

She'd taken some walks there when she'd worked for the gallery. She'd gone there often to clear her head. To get away from the terrible John Abram who'd hired her not for her brain but for her looks.

Minutes ticked by.

Sarah glanced at her watch. It was just after eleven.

Behind her, Buzz let out a whine. She turned toward him and rubbed his head.

"What is it, boy?"

He whined again.

That's when she realized that he probably had to go to the bathroom. They'd been in the truck for a long time. And Buzz had eaten the same dog food every day without change for the past four years. The unexpected change in his meals was bound to upset his stomach.

Sarah frowned. "Can't you wait for Colton to get back?"

He barked.

"No, hush." She tried to silence him by rubbing his head. "Don't draw any attention to us."

He barked again, louder this time. The canine probably sensed her panic, which only added to his anxiety right now.

This wasn't good.

Sarah glanced around. One person—a businessman with a briefcase—glanced their way.

"What are you doing, Buzz?" she murmured. "You're going to have to wait. You can do that, can't you?"

He barked even louder.

Buzz couldn't wait, Sarah realized. He was going to keep barking until he got out to relieve himself.

With a tremble raking through her hands, Sarah knew she was going to have to leave the truck for a moment. She couldn't risk Buzz drawing too much attention to them with his barking. Besides, it was cruel to make him hold it.

She glanced around and still saw no one suspicious.

With trepidation, Sarah opened her door, bracing herself to venture out for a few minutes.

She hoped she wouldn't regret this.

NINE

Colton waited for a moment in the lobby as the receptionist called up to Debbie Wilcox.

The office of Blanchard Pharmaceuticals had spared no expense with this building. The walls appeared to be marble and all the decorations were slick. The atmosphere contained an air of professionalism—and mourning. Numerous people had walked past with tissues in their hands, whispering quiet condolences to any and everyone they passed.

As he waited, he put in a call to Goodwind's Jewelry. Though he wanted to believe Sarah, he wanted to verify what she'd told him. Sure enough. She did have an appointment there today.

Relief swept through him.

Good. He felt better knowing Sarah was being open with him.

A few minutes later, Colton was called up to Debbie's office. The mood around him seemed even more somber on this floor. Was everyone here mourning the death of their CEO? Were they trying to regroup? Were they theorizing about what had happened?

At the direction of a receptionist, Colton walked down a short hallway, knocked on a door and then stepped into an office. A woman sat behind a desk there, a pile of tissues filling the trash can beside her chair.

Debbie Wilcox was probably in her late thirties with dark hair, stylish glasses and a trim business suit. She looked up from her desk and offered a professional smile. But her red eyes showed she'd taken Loretta's death hard also.

"How can I help you?" she asked, lacing her fingers together.

Colton stood in front of her and paused. "I'm looking into the death of Loretta Blanchard, and I'm hoping you can help me."

Debbie balled another tissue in her hands before raising an eyebrow. "And you are?"

"I'm Colton Hawk. I'm a former Seattle detective." He pulled out his ID and showed her. "I don't have a badge, but I can assure you that I'm legit."

She took his ID from him and examined it a moment before handing it back. With a touch of weariness in her voice, she asked, "What do you need to know? I thought the police already had a suspect. That's what the news is making it sound like."

"They do have a person of interest, but I believe they should look into other possibilities, as well."

She leaned back in her leather chair and crossed her arms, almost seeming resigned. "Whatever you need to know. Loretta was a good woman, and she'll be missed by everyone here. Her death is a huge loss to the medical community."

It sounded like a standard public relations script. Colton needed more than that. "Did she have any enemies?"

"Any enemies?" Debbie thought about it for a moment, ignoring the phone as it rang on her desk. "I think *enemy* would be a strong word. Loretta was a hard woman to love. She was smart, confident and brisk. She didn't let people into her inner circle. People admired her, but I'm not sure many wanted to be her friend."

"I see." Colton could easily picture the kind of woman Loretta was. He'd met the type before. And the description matched what Sarah had already told him.

"Did she make anyone mad?"

Debbie shrugged. "There are people she's fired throughout the years. But more recently, she had other people handling those kinds of unpleasant situations for her. Although, I can make you a list, if that would help."

"It would."

"I suppose she also had competitors. I wouldn't say enemies, but as I'm sure you probably know, the drug business is big business."

"So I've heard."

"I'd say our biggest competition here at Blanchard Pharmaceuticals would have to be the folks over at Danson Tech."

Danson Tech? Colton vaguely recognized their name. Maybe from a commercial on TV or something? "Where is Danson Tech based out of?"

"It's funny, actually. They're based out of Coeur d'Alene. It's unusual to have two companies so close together, but the company's founder, Yvonne Warner, was actually Loretta's roommate while in college."

"Isn't that interesting." Colton had no idea they had such a personal connection. That very well could lead to Yvonne being his number-one suspect.

Debbie raised her eyebrows. "It is, isn't it? And if you're wondering if Yvonne is responsible, you should know that she was out of the country helping sick children in Africa. It's been documented all over the web."

"Good to know." He had thought about seeking her out

next. At least he could save some time and not do that—after he verified the information.

She sat up and straightened some papers on her desk, a silent cue that she was ready to wrap up this conversation. "Other than that, I'm not sure. Loretta didn't talk about her personal life very often. Now I can see I should have pressed more. Maybe if I had, this wouldn't have happened." The woman's facade cracked as her eyes filled with moisture.

"What do you mean?" Colton asked, his curiosity spiking.

"I just mean that it's a shame the woman had to hire someone," Debbie said. "Loretta paid that woman to do things a friend should have been able to do for her—help with groceries, housework, act as a companion. She worked hard for her entire life, but it boiled down to her having no one. It's sad, really."

"It does seem unfortunate, especially for someone who was so esteemed in the community."

"She told me one time that I should hold my friends close but my enemies closer. It's an old saying, I know. But when Loretta said it, she looked like she meant it. Like she'd lived it."

That was interesting. Just what kind of enemies did Loretta have? And which ones had been disguised as friends? "That's good to know. Thanks so much for your time."

Colton had stepped away when Debbie called him back. He paused and turned toward her.

Debbie's gaze locked on to his. "I hope you find whoever did this to her. And if you need anything else, don't hesitate to call. Everyone here wants to figure this out and see Loretta get the justice she deserves."

Sarah tugged on Buzz's leash and glanced around the city sidewalk.

No one appeared to be watching them—that she could

see. Still, she had to play it safe. There was too much at stake right now.

She pushed her sunglasses up higher, tugged her baseball cap down lower and led Buzz to the park.

She wished she could call Colton and tell him where she was going. But she no longer had a phone. Hopefully, she'd let Buzz go do his business and then return before Colton got back.

There were no green areas around here, which only left the park. It wasn't far away—it was a block away. And although the day was brisk, thankfully she had her coat on.

Colton's coat.

When she pulled it close, she caught whiffs of his scent. His leathery aftershave.

How she missed that scent. How she missed Colton.

The thought nearly stopped her cold. No, she didn't miss Colton. She missed the *idea* of what they could have been. But she was better off alone. Better off not getting her heart broken again.

Sarah and Buzz reached a lovely park filled with walking trails, a river and a little playground.

"Go ahead, Buzz," she murmured. "We don't have much time."

As the dog sniffed around, Sarah remained on guard for any signs of trouble.

She'd seen that man standing over Loretta. Sarah had gotten to her room too late—he'd already given her that fatal wound. Sarah knew he wouldn't hesitate to do the same to her. Her only comfort was that she was in public. Certainly there was some safety to be found in that.

Despite her reassurances, her arms still trembled.

It was too bad, really. This place was so beautiful.

Sarah had always wanted to come here and practice her watercolors. At the time, she'd felt like the future was flung wide open ahead of her with grand possibilities waiting at every turn. No longer.

Now, her future seemed bleaker than the gray day around her.

Buzz sniffed around the grass, around a tree.

Sarah silently willed the dog to hurry up. But she knew it would do no good. Soon enough, Buzz would do his business, and they could return to the truck, to safety.

Buzz pulled her farther down a walking trail and finally paused beside a tree.

As Sarah waited, her skin crawled, and she swung her head around.

Was that her internal instincts telling her that something was wrong?

She didn't know for sure, but she didn't want to take any chances.

"Come on, Buzz."

Sarah glanced around again but saw no one suspicious. A businessman strolling with a phone to his ear. A mother chasing two young children. Another man walking his dog.

Everything seemed normal.

Just as the thought entered her mind, Buzz let out a low growl.

Even Buzz knew something was wrong.

But what? What—or who—was the source of this danger?

Sarah tugged on Buzz's leash, suddenly anxious to leave. "We need to get out of here, boy."

But as she started back toward the truck, she heard a bullet whiz past her.

Someone was shooting at her, she realized. And the shot had narrowly missed her.

That time.

TEN

Colton glanced around as he left the building for Blanchard Pharmaceuticals.

While his talk with Debbie Wilcox hadn't been overly enlightening, he had gotten some insight as to Loretta's personal life—or lack thereof. The woman was brilliant but lonely. A genius yet difficult. A force to be reckoned with and someone a person didn't want to get on the bad side of.

He still needed to remain on guard right now. Though he'd lost the person following them earlier, this guy who'd killed Loretta and who was now chasing them obviously had resources. It was the only way he'd be able to track Sarah's phone and follow them.

Colton knew they needed to stay on the move if they were to stay alive—which was why he was anxious to get back to Sarah right now.

As soon as he saw his truck parked at the curb, he sucked in a breath.

Why didn't he see Sarah or Buzz? Were they slumped down low?

His gut told him no, told him that they were gone. But he needed to confirm before acting on anything.

Colton quickened his steps even more. As he reached his truck, he peered inside. It was just like he thought: empty.

What had happened to them?

He glanced around the sidewalks at the crowds who wandered from place to place. The businesspeople. The shoppers. A few college students.

There was no sight of Sarah or Buzz. Sarah might blend in, but Colton would spot that husky anywhere—yet Buzz was nowhere to be seen.

Jogging, Colton hurried to the intersection and glanced down the street.

They weren't there either.

Sarah and Buzz couldn't have gone but so far. Colton was only inside the building for fifteen minutes, and there was no sign of a struggle in his vehicle.

His gaze scanned the signs in front of him.

The Riverfront.

Would Sarah have taken Buzz there? It was worth checking out.

Colton's jog became a run as he hurried down the street. With each step, his apprehension grew until his muscles felt tight enough to break.

Please, Lord, let Sarah be okay. Buzz too. I don't know why You brought Sarah back into my life, but whatever the reason, don't snatch her away yet. Please.

Colton dodged across the street and stopped in the middle of a grassy area. He desperately hoped to find Sarah and Buzz here.

Still not spotting them, he darted toward a walking trail in the distance. As he did, he heard barking.

Buzz?

It had to be.

He quickened his steps, but another sound sliced through the air.

Gunfire.

People around him screamed and ran away.

He had to find Sarah.

Now.

Just as he stepped onto the other side of some bushes, he spotted Sarah. Terror stretched across her face as she turned toward something in the distance.

Just as another bullet rang out, Buzz jumped on her, pushing Sarah to the ground, to safety.

But Colton had a feeling this wasn't over yet.

Sarah hit the icy ground just as another bullet whizzed past. Her heart pounded out of control as she waited for what would happen next. Buzz stood on top of her, a low growl emerging from deep in his chest.

People around her ran, scattered, fled for their lives.

She needed to run, but she was too scared to rise. Fear paralyzed her. Fear of running. Fear of staying.

She should have never left the truck.

"Sarah, are you okay?" someone whispered above her.

She looked up.

Colton…he'd found her. He knelt beside her now, but his gaze remained fixated on something in the distance.

The shooter, she realized.

She nodded quickly, fearing for Colton's safety. "I'm fine."

"Buzz, stay with her," Colton said. "Meet me back at the truck in five."

He took off in a run toward the trees.

He was going after the shooter, Sarah realized.

Oh, dear Lord. Watch over him. End this nightmare. I beg You.

As she heard frosty foliage rustling in the distance, she realized the shooter was running.

She nudged Buzz off from atop her and stood, wiping the snow from her knees.

"Are you okay?" a woman asked, keeping her distance yet her eyes filled with concern.

Sarah nodded, trying not to draw any attention to herself. That was the last thing she wanted—for someone to recognize her. "Yes… I'm fine. Thank you."

She had to get out of here. Now. Before the cops showed up.

She couldn't go to jail for Loretta's murder. Not right now especially. She needed answers first, and she wouldn't find them in a cell.

Colton had said to meet at his truck. That's what she needed to do.

With another nervous glance around, she grabbed Buzz's leash. They began walking at a brisk pace down the sidewalk. Sarah wanted to run, but stopped herself, giving a silent reminder that she should attempt to blend in.

The Riverfront area felt strangely normal and unaffected considering what had just happened. A few people still fled from the scene. Others were clueless about the gunshots that had rung out. Others moved on briskly, acting as if their schedules were too busy to be bothered by a crime that they had no direct involvement in.

Sarah couldn't see the area where Colton had run.

Had he caught the man? What if the man had caught Colton?

Panic tried to swell in her, but Sarah attempted to hold it at bay.

Instead, she glanced again at the winter wonderland around them. Her breath came out in icy poofs in front of her face.

It appeared the situation had de-escalated. People's panic had quickly receded, other than a few who had been right there.

No one looked at her now. All the people who'd been there during the shooting seemed to have scattered.

In the distance, sirens wailed louder.

The cops were on their way. If they saw her…

Sarah picked up her pace.

She walked the first block, each step feeling safer. She knew she couldn't let down her guard, though. Too much was at stake.

Finally, she reached the truck without incident. She and Buzz climbed into the front seat and ducked down low, so they wouldn't be spotted. But, at any minute, Sarah half expected the gunman to find her. To knock at her window. For a bullet to shatter the glass above her.

No, she couldn't think like that. She just needed to wait for Colton.

Where was he?

What would Sarah do if Colton didn't get back? She didn't care about the man romantically anymore, but she didn't want something to happen to him.

Or *did* she still care about him? Had she ever stopped?

Her heartbeat sounded like a deafening throb in her ears.

She'd have to think about that at another time. Right now, she needed to focus on surviving. She petted Buzz's head as he lay in the back of the truck beside her. Thank goodness the windows were tinted, offering another layer of concealment.

The police sirens wailed closer.

Sarah held her breath, desperate to know if the police were coming for her. If someone had secretly been watching and reported her. Panic climbed higher and higher until she felt like she couldn't breathe.

In only a few seconds, she'd learn whether the police were coming for her or not.

The sirens wailed closer…and kept going.

Sarah released her breath.

Thank You, God.

As she shifted on the floor, something pressed into her side.

The truck keys Colton had given to her. He'd told her to leave if she had to.

Would that be now?

But she didn't want to leave Colton behind. What if she couldn't find him? What if he was hurt? Arrested?

Jitters filled her stomach.

She needed to make a decision and quickly.

Just then, the driver's side door jerked open.

Sarah craned her neck to get a glimpse of who it was, fearing it might be the killer. The police. Instead, it was Colton.

Steely eyed. Jaw set with determination. Movements confident but urgent.

And he looked okay. He was alive and unharmed.

Her shoulders sagged with relief.

She handed him the keys, and he jammed them into the ignition.

Two seconds later, they took off, headed away from trouble...hopefully.

ELEVEN

Colton pulled off from the curb where he'd parked, desperate to get away before anyone saw them and pointed them out to the cops. His hands were white-knuckled on the steering wheel as he wove between cars on the street, his mind racing as he processed what happened.

"Why in the world did you get out of the truck, Sarah?" As the question left his lips, Colton glanced in the rearview mirror, searching for police cars or the black sedan from earlier.

He saw nothing.

"Buzz…he had to go to the bathroom," Sarah said, stroking the dog's head. "He started barking, and I was afraid he was going to draw attention to us. I didn't know what else to do, and I couldn't call you. I'm sorry."

Hearing the sincerity of Sarah's words eased some of the tension in Colton's shoulders. "It's okay. I'm not blaming you. I just… I just thought you were gone."

"Thank you for actually looking for me when you could have easily just let me go."

There was something in Sarah's tone that made Colton pause.

Did she think Colton had let her go too easily before? Did she think it was easy to watch her walk away? Because it had torn him up inside—torn him up for months until he'd lost weight and hardly been able to sleep.

But this wasn't the time to talk about those things, not when their lives were on the line. Their past could wait.

"Did you see the man who shot at me?" Sarah asked.

Colton's jaw clenched tighter as he remembered the chase. As he remembered rushing across the icy ground, trying to capture the shooter. For a moment, he'd felt so close. "There was a car waiting on the other side of those trees. He jumped inside and sped off."

Sarah frowned. "Same car that followed us?"

"Yes, it was."

"So he somehow found us."

"Or maybe he assumed you might come here." Colton's words rang out in the truck.

"I don't even know who this person is. I don't know how he can predict anything about where I am." Sarah glanced at Colton, her eyes full of questions. "What about Debbie? Did she tell you anything?"

Colton wished he had more to share, that they'd made more progress during these first few hours. "Just that Loretta was a bit of a loner."

"That's right. She was. She enjoyed being by herself. That's what she said, at least."

"Now that you've had more time to think about it, did Loretta talk about anyone? Talk to anyone?"

Sarah shrugged, then shook her head. "The landscaper maybe. She loved talking about flowers and herbs with him."

"Who's the landscaper?"

"His name is…" Sarah paused again and then snapped her fingers. "Frank Mills. He was always working outside. He would probably have some insight into things—into Loretta."

It was a place to start, at least. "Any idea where this Frank Mills lives?"

"Actually, I do remember. He lives in Bellamy Acres on the north side of town. I only remember because one of the artists at the last gallery I worked at lives there. Despite the name, it's full of little craftsman-style houses on small lots."

"Maybe we should pay him a visit," Colton said. "See what he knows."

"I think that's a great idea. But if he sees me…" Sarah's voice grew distant, and Colton heard the tremble there.

"We need to convince him you're not guilty."

Sarah nodded. "I'm game. I just want this to be over. I want answers. And I want to stop living in fear."

"Then let's do this."

Sarah's hands felt sweaty as they pulled into Frank's neighborhood. It was just like she remembered it—full of character yet understated. She always thought that if she was able to buy a house, she'd like one like this. She wanted something cozy and warm.

Or like Colton's place with its high ceiling, log beams and natural stone fireplace.

The thought surprised her. But his cabin had felt homey, and it had been nice to breathe the fresh air. To see nothing but mountains. To feel like the world wasn't closing in on her.

Sarah never wanted a lot in life. She didn't care about being rich or acquiring material things. But she did value security. Having a safe place to live. She'd had so very few of those things.

Everything Sarah held close—what little she had—had been turned upside down. Or stripped away. It was like she'd always known that she only had herself to depend on.

"Looks like Buzz was a lifesaver back there," Colton said, glancing behind him.

Sarah followed his gaze and rubbed Buzz's head as he panted beside her. "Yes, he really was. It was like he sensed danger was close. In fact, I might not be around right now if it wasn't for Buzz. He pushed me out of harm's way."

"He's a smart dog. You can see it in his eyes."

"Loretta picked him, and she was a smart lady."

"She picked you too." Colton stole a glance at her.

Sarah shrugged, wishing she could believe Colton's words. But she felt so worn down. Like she'd made so many bad decisions. And now everyone thought she'd killed Loretta. When would she ever catch a break?

"I mean it, Sarah," Colton continued. "Loretta chose you for a reason. She saw something in you."

"Thanks." Her throat ached as the words left her lips. His words had touched her more than she anticipated. Just having someone who believed in her, it meant more than she wanted to acknowledge.

Why was Colton being so nice to her now? It reminded her of when they'd first started to date. She'd been over-the-moon happy to be with him. Those months were some of the best of her life, leading right up to the moment Colton had proposed to her.

Then Colton had been forced to shoot the intoxicated, belligerent man on his last case. Colton had become withdrawn. Distant. He stopped opening up to her and wanted to spend more time by himself. And he always got that distant look in his eyes, like he was physically with her but not mentally or emotionally.

Sarah was able to see the writing on the wall. She'd sensed the change.

It wasn't that he was mean. Colton wasn't that kind of guy. But he'd definitely pulled away.

Just like her dad had pulled away before he left Sarah's life forever. She couldn't put herself through that again.

She *wouldn't*.

Colton pulled to a stop in front of Frank's home—they'd looked up his address on the way here—and put the truck in Park. Sarah glanced over at the house. The cozy-looking home was painted white with blue shutters. Snow surrounded the structure, and all it needed was smoke puffing from the chimney, and it would have looked like it belonged in a storybook.

Behind the house, she barely caught a glimpse of the snow-capped mountains that she so dearly loved. They could inspire a thousand paintings, and then some.

"I think you should come with me to talk to Frank," Colton said.

Surprise raced through her. "If the police see me with you, your career could be in jeopardy, Colton."

"I can handle whatever is thrown at me."

She raised her eyebrows, surprised that Colton was willing to risk so much. Should she even let him? She didn't know. Instead, she said, "Thank you, Colton."

"It's no problem." He nodded toward the door, always the perfect gentleman—the ideal mix of tough and tender. "Now let's go see if we can find some answers."

She climbed out behind him and called Buzz. The dog trotted out from the truck and fell into step beside her, nuzzling the snow before sneezing.

Buzz had always seemed to love these conditions. Sarah remembered him frolicking outside on more than one occasion. But not now. Buzz seemed to know—to sense—everything that was going on.

Another rush of nerves went through Sarah as they climbed onto the porch and a chilly breeze swept over the landscape, invading her clothing until she shivered again.

Colton rang the front bell, and they waited. Sarah glanced around, anxiety continuing to rise with every second that passed.

Frank's truck was in the driveway. He was obviously home. So why wasn't he answering the door? Had he spotted them through the window and called the police?

Sarah glanced at Colton. He didn't seem nervous.

She really should follow his lead and try to remain calm in this trying situation.

Except she and Colton were opposites. They always had been. Sarah was the emotional, intuitive one. Colton had been the calm, logical thinker. At one time, she'd thought they complemented each other perfectly.

The sound of the doorbell chiming inside drew her attention back to the present. Two more attempts later, no one answered.

Colton turned to her. "Let's check around back, just in case."

Sarah glanced at the beautifully manicured flower beds as they passed. Frank definitely had a gift for working with plants. Even in the winter, they looked lovely with the evergreens he'd chosen and artfully arranged.

She knew the man was single, but she wasn't sure if he had any kids or not. Frank never talked about them, and gardening seemed to be his life. He'd come across as nice and friendly—more welcoming than most of the people in Loretta's world.

Sarah followed Colton on the sidewalk to the back of the house, her boots crunching on the icy snow.

The only other prints out here were hers, Colton's, and Buzz's. However, a fresh snow had fallen last night, so maybe Frank hadn't left his house all day. Maybe he'd heard about Loretta and had taken some time to mourn.

Sarah paused just for a minute as she stepped into the

backyard. This area looked just as lovely as the front, including a gazebo and a little bridge that crossed what must be a man-made pond that had now frozen over.

"This is fabulous, isn't it?" Sarah murmured aloud, her artist's mind already painting pictures of it.

"Yes, it really is. He has a gift, for sure, and I can see why Loretta chose him." Colton kept walking toward the garage on the other side of the yard.

"I think that's why I liked Frank so much. He and I both had an artistic side to us, you know?"

"I can see that." Colton paused by the garage door. "Let me just check inside. If he's not there, we'll move on."

"Okay."

Sarah followed behind Colton, but nearly collided with him at the garage door.

"What's wrong?" Sarah asked, trying to peer over his shoulder.

Colton held his hand up, stopping Sarah from going any farther.

"No wonder he didn't answer the door," Colton said.

Sarah scooted around him, desperate to see with her own eyes what he was talking about.

Frank lay on the floor of his garage, blood seeping from what appeared to be a bullet wound in his chest.

Her hand went over her mouth to cover the O of horror there. No, not Frank…not another person who'd lost his life…

Nausea roiled in her gut as the direness of the situation hit her full force.

How were they ever going to get out of this alive?

TWELVE

Colton's stomach tightened as he knelt on the frigid cement floor of the garage beside Frank's prone body. He touched the man's wrist, feeling for a pulse. As Colton suspected, there was none.

His skin was cold—ice-cold. Based on how the man looked, Colton would guess that he'd probably been dead several hours already. Even his blood, pooled on the floor, had frozen.

A gun lay beside him, near his hand, almost like he'd dropped it.

Frank looked like he was probably in his early sixties with gray hair and a fit build. He didn't have the face of a killer—not that that meant anything. No, he looked like a grandfather.

"Did he kill himself?" Sarah asked, her hand still over her mouth, covering the horror on her face. She'd seen two dead people within the past twenty-four hours, and she'd probably never seen a murder victim until then. This was bound to be hard on her.

Colton stood and stared down at Frank, his chest tightening at what seemed like such a senseless act, whether it was suicide or murder. "I don't know. The gun makes it appear that way, doesn't it?"

Sarah cast a sharp glance his way. "Wait, do you think someone set him up?"

Colton's jaw tightened. "I'm not assuming anything right now. But I need to let the police know what's going on."

"The police?" Panic laced her voice. "But you can't call the police."

Colton knew how delicate this situation was, and he was torn between his duty as a former cop and his loyalty toward the woman who'd broken his heart. Above all, he had to do the right thing. That was most important.

"I'm going to have to take you and Buzz somewhere safe," Colton finally said, after thinking things through for a minute. "But, Sarah, I can't not report this. Every second counts when it comes to a crime like this. If someone killed Frank, time is of the essence."

"I understand." Her voice sounded compassionate and resolute but also fearful.

It was understandable. Anyone in her shoes—falsely accused of murder and the target of a killer—should feel a good dose of fear.

"I'll make sure you're secure first, okay?" Colton told her.

He would do everything within his power to make sure that Sarah didn't get hurt. To ensure that she was protected and safe. Heartbroken or not, he couldn't live with himself if he allowed harm to come to her.

Sarah nodded but looked unconvinced.

This wasn't the way Colton liked to do things, but he didn't have much of a choice right now. He had to protect Sarah—but he also had to act as an officer of the law.

"The sooner we go, the better," Colton said. "I want to keep things on the up-and-up as much as I can."

Sarah's gaze remained fixated on Frank, her skin growing paler every second she stood there. Buzz nuzzled her hand, as if trying to cheer her up.

Colton needed to get her out of here before the trauma of the situation hit her even harder. The sooner they left, the better. "Let's go."

He placed a hand on her back to lead her away, afraid she might pass out. But she kept moving, one foot in front of the other—almost robotically—until they reached his vehicle.

They climbed back in Colton's truck. He'd find a hotel for her to stay in, and once he knew she was safe, he'd come back out here.

For now, he started the ignition and pulled out of the neighborhood. He'd need to go somewhere secluded, somewhere Sarah would be a safe enough distance from this whole mess, just in case things went south.

"I can't believe he's dead," Sarah said as she sat beside him, looking dazed. Maybe even in shock.

But at least she was talking. It was when Sarah stopped communicating and started to bottle everything up inside that he got worried. That was what had happened right before she'd left. It was like she'd made her mind up, that she'd buried her fears and concerns, and self-preservation had won out.

Against Colton's better instincts, he reached over and squeezed Sarah's hand. He tried to let go, but he couldn't. Something about feeling her fingers in his brought back better memories of their past—the memories that he missed. Memories of the good times. Memories he should try to forget.

"I'm sorry you had to see that, Sarah," he said softly.

"This is bad, Colton." She squeezed his hand also, not looking the least bit inclined to let go. She probably wasn't thinking clearly or she would have.

In the meantime, he wouldn't argue. It felt good to feel

her soft fingers intertwined with his—if only briefly. He'd
never admitted it, but he missed these moments.

He missed Sarah.

"I know," Colton finally said. "It is bad."

There was no need to skirt around the truth. They
were both in an impossible situation right now, and it was
going to take every ounce of their strength and wits to get
through it.

"I didn't want any of this," she continued. "All I wanted
was…"

"What did you want, Sarah?" Colton honestly needed
to know. He'd asked himself that question about Sarah for
two years now. He just couldn't figure out her endgame.

"I wanted a safe place," she said quietly.

"I wasn't safe?" Colton hadn't meant for the question
to slip out, but it had.

"Colton—" She started to explain.

Before she got any further with whatever she was about
to say, Colton realized what a mistake that might be to
continue this conversation. "Never mind. It's okay. I don't
know why I asked."

He pulled into the parking lot of a cheap motel with
outside entrances for each room—which would probably
work in their favor—especially with Buzz.

Sarah opened her mouth like she might respond but shut
it again. It was just as well. Because there was nothing she
could say that would change things. No, the damage had
already been done, and there was no reversing it as far as
Colton was concerned.

Sarah leaned back on the bed, biding her time until
Colton returned. Buzz seemed to feel the same way. He
looked rather mopey as he lay at her feet. He wasn't relaxing; it was almost like he was pretending to for her sake.

"You're a good boy," she murmured, stroking his head. "You've been my saving grace. What would I do without you?"

He nuzzled her hand.

"You've always been there for me." Her words were true. Throughout everything that had happened, Buzz had been the one she shared her deepest secrets with as she took him on walks and brushed his fur. He'd almost become like a best friend.

"You know about all my mistakes and you still love me," she continued. "And you know what? I can't see you ever leaving me. I can't say that about many people."

He let out a long sigh.

She rubbed his head once more before glancing around.

She hated this hotel already. It smelled old, like a mix of dust and mildew. The quilt on the bed was probably thirty years old with an orange-and-brown pattern. The carpet was matted, beige and stained.

At least the location was off the beaten path. Woods and mountains lined the back of it, and a small stream, now frozen, had at one time cascaded along the edge of the property.

There were more glimpses here of God's majesty. They were everywhere when people just opened their eyes to it. But even despite that reminder, Sarah still felt an unrest at being here alone while Colton went out to take the bullets for her.

She wished she had a cell phone or computer or…that she could do something.

But there was nothing to do but wait.

Every time she closed her eyes, she saw images of Frank. Dead. With blood on his chest.

Poor Frank.

Poor Loretta.

Whatever was going on here, it was bigger than Sarah had ever imagined.

And now she was in the middle of it.

She glanced at her watch. Colton had been gone an hour. What was taking so long? What if he never returned? What if he turned her in and told the police she was here?

No, Sarah couldn't think like that. Because no matter what their past history was, Colton wasn't that kind of guy.

Although she would still love to know what was going on.

But she didn't have her phone anymore. She had no way of communicating or even checking in on the outside world.

At the thought of it, she straightened. A memory hit her.

Loretta had sent her an email yesterday evening. Sarah had been at the art show. She'd only glanced at her inbox and had seen the email come in. She hadn't bothered to check it and had told herself she would do so later.

What if Loretta had emailed her something that would give insight about what had happened to her? This could be the breakthrough they'd been looking for.

But how was Sarah going to get that email?

She nibbled on the inside of her lip as she thought through the question.

There had been a computer in an office beside the reception area of the motel. It was the kind meant for businessmen and women or travelers who needed to print tickets and such.

If Sarah could get there and hop on really quick, then maybe she could discover something.

She glanced at Buzz. "What do you think, buddy?"

He stared at her.

He clearly thought it was a bad idea.

But that didn't deter Sarah.

Maybe she just needed something to do to keep her mind occupied. Maybe this was the clue they'd been looking for.

"I can't take you with me," she muttered, rubbing the dog's head. "Can you stay here and be a good boy?"

Buzz whined, as if he understood.

"I'll only be a minute. I promise."

He whined again. Even Buzz thought this was a dangerous plan.

She wanted to read that email. And what better time than now while Colton was occupied?

Sarah had been checking out the window. No one was here. No one knew she was here. Besides, she'd only be a minute, and this could help with their investigation.

With a new resolve, Sarah stood and grabbed the key card to the room. She gave Buzz one last pat on the head and then stepped outside.

Looking both ways, she saw no one.

Carefully, Sarah hurried across the sidewalk toward the lobby. She pulled her hat down lower as she stepped inside, nodded at the man behind the desk, and then she slipped into the room with the computer.

Perfect. No one else was here.

Quickly, she pulled up her emails, desperate to see if there was a clue there she'd missed earlier.

But as soon as the screen filled with her messages, her eyes went to the newest one.

It was from the storage facility where she kept her paintings. The building flooded after the recent snow and rain, and she needed to go check on her items.

Her stomach clenched. Had her paintings been ruined?

Tears pressed at her eyes. She didn't want to cry. There were far more important matters to cry about. But those watercolors represented years of work.

If they were destroyed, then Sarah really wouldn't have anything left, would she?

As she noticed movement out front, she glanced over at the glass doors.

A black sedan pulled up.

Was it the man who'd been following them?

She didn't know for sure. But Sarah did know she had to get out of here. Now.

THIRTEEN

Sarah found a back exit and slipped outside. Woods and a small creek lined the back side of the building. Here, she was concealed—but also more isolated if the man found her.

Careful to remain out of sight and moving quickly, she skirted around the side of the building until she reached the corner. She pressed herself against the wall and peered around to the front parking lot.

The sedan was still there, outside near the front door.

Had the man gone inside? Was he questioning the clerk, asking if he'd seen her?

Sarah knew the most likely answer was yes.

She didn't have much time.

She had to get to Buzz.

Sarah darted to her room. Her hands trembled as she jammed the key card into the lock. She glanced back one more time as the door opened.

A man stepped out of the lobby. Sarah couldn't make out much about him except that he was large—muscular—and he wore aviator shades. His dark hair was slicked back from his face.

She didn't think she'd ever seen the man before.

That had to be the person following her. He was large enough to be the killer.

He hadn't seen her. Not yet.

But Sarah knew he'd probably check all of these rooms until he found her and killed her.

She locked the door. And then she shoved a chair in front of it. Adrenaline pulsed through her blood.

Buzz rushed toward her, his body on alert as his canine intuition reared to life.

Sarah glanced around.

How was she going to get out of here?

There were no windows other than those at the front of the room.

They weren't a possibility. And there was no other way out.

Fighting panic, she glanced out the window. The man was walking toward her room.

He'd seen her. Knew she was here.

And he was coming for her.

"Buzz, we've got to do something," Sarah whispered, her head swirling with adrenaline and fear. "But what?"

Buzz walked toward the interior door by the TV and he sat there. It was the passageway leading to the adjoining room for families or groups that needed more than one area.

"I should go into the connecting room?" It seemed like a good enough idea. Besides, it wasn't like Sarah had many other options right now.

She opened the door on her side of the space and listened for a moment. It was silent on the other side. Maybe that meant the room was unoccupied. She hadn't heard any noises coming from the space since she'd arrived.

Moving quickly, Sarah grabbed the other knob.

It was locked.

How was she going to get this open?

Could she charge the door and knock it down? She doubted she was strong enough. Besides, it would be too noisy. Certainly the man would hear her.

There had to be something else she could do.

She pulled out her key card. She'd only ever seen this done on TV. Would it work in real life?

Someone banged on her door just then. "Maintenance!"

Sarah had no choice but to find out if her theory would work. The man was here and only moments away from killing her.

She jammed the card where the lock was, praying it would release.

Please, Lord. Please. Let this work!

Her hand still shook uncontrollably. That didn't stop her. She continued to jam the card into the lock mechanism, hoping—praying—it would catch.

The man knocked again. Then something crashed into the door.

He was trying to get into her room, she realized. And nothing was going to stop him.

Sarah gave the card one last shove.

Something gave.

She sucked in a breath.

It had worked, she realized. The card had released the latch!

Sarah pushed the door open, hoping no one else was on the other side who would alert the man about what she'd done.

Quickly, she scanned the space. The room—identical to her own—appeared empty.

"Come on, Buzz," she whispered. She clucked her tongue once. It was Loretta's command for him to come.

As trained, the dog ran inside. Sarah grabbed Buzz's

bag, flung it on her back, and shut the doors quietly. She hoped to conceal what she'd done and buy herself some time.

Just as the door clicked closed behind her, a crash sounded from her room.

The man must have kicked open her door.

Sarah had escaped just in time.

But this wasn't over yet. No, Sarah needed to think and act quickly if she wanted to get out of this alive.

Colton's head pounded as he headed down the road from Frank's house.

He'd just spent the past hour and a half talking to police and trying to explain himself. Explaining how he'd found Frank.

He'd told investigators that he'd decided to look into the case himself as a personal favor to a friend who just happened to be their prime suspect. Again he'd been warned that Sarah might not be who he remembered.

He didn't believe that. She was the same Sarah, only a little more broken than before. More than anything, Colton wished he could help put her back together. But it wasn't his place. Not anymore. He'd help her through this situation, and then his life would return to normal. He had no other choice.

But his heart seemed to be telling him otherwise, despite all his logic.

The one piece of good news he'd received was that the police had talked to John Abram, the man Sarah had worked for who'd accused her of stealing. He'd confessed that she was innocent, and he'd made the story up.

Colton pulled up to the hotel and froze. A black sedan was parked in front of the lobby area.

His breath hitched.

It was the man who'd been following them earlier. The killer.

He'd found them again somehow.

Had he already gotten Sarah and Buzz?

Colton sped toward his room and threw his truck into Park. Just as he drew his gun, he saw the curtain move in the room beside theirs.

A familiar face peeked out.

That was Sarah.

She saw him and threw the door open.

The next instant, she and Buzz darted across the sidewalk and dove into his truck.

"Go!" Sarah yelled. "Go!"

Colton didn't ask any questions. He pressed the accelerator and his engine revved as they raced toward the road. Just as they reached the blacktop, Colton looked back.

A man wearing a black leather coat stepped from his room and stared after them.

They should be a safe enough distance away to lose him.

But Colton had to be certain. He couldn't take a chance on Sarah's life.

He took a sharp right turn and headed back into the city. He needed to disappear among the traffic there.

He glanced in his rearview mirror again.

He didn't see the sedan.

Thank goodness. Maybe they'd gotten enough of a head start.

"What happened back there?" Colton asked.

Sarah shook her head, her cheeks flushed and her chest rising and falling too rapidly. "I don't know. I saw the man pull up and panicked. I knew I had to do something. Buzz went right to the door between the two rooms, and I knew that was my only option. I managed to get the door open. It's a good thing you pulled up when you did, though..."

"Yeah, it is." Colton had come close to losing her, and he could barely stomach the thought.

Right now, he wanted nothing more than to pull Sarah into his arms and hold her. To tell her that everything would be okay. To whisk her off somewhere she'd be safe.

But none of those things were options. No, he had to stay focused here. Stay logical. And to forget about their past and all the old feelings that wanted to bubble to the surface.

Instead, Colton glanced behind him again. He still didn't see the sedan. Maybe they'd finally caught a break.

"I don't know how this guy is finding us, but he is," Colton said.

"I know. I don't like it. Not at all."

Colton's thoughts raced. Where else could this guy have left a tracker or found a means of trailing them?

As he glanced at Buzz, an idea hit him. "What's that thing on Buzz's collar?"

Sarah reached for the collar and touched the tag there. But she felt something behind it. "What is that, boy?"

She slipped the collar off and pulled it toward her for examination. Then she let out a gasp. "It's a tracker, the kind you can put on your keys so you won't lose them. It should be linked to a phone."

"This guy must have known about it." Colton shook his head. "That's how he's been tracking us. He has Loretta's phone, after all."

"What do we do?"

"Throw it out the window."

Sarah glanced at him, making sure she'd understood correctly. "Really?"

"Yes, really. We'll get Buzz a new one."

She rolled down the window and tossed it into the woods. A moment of silence fell between them, and Sarah shivered. Finally, she asked, "Did you find out anything at Frank's?"

"Not a lot. But I got confirmation that Randolph Stephens's car was stolen about a week ago."

Sarah's shoulders sagged. "So the vehicle that was following us wasn't him?"

"No, it wasn't."

"What about Frank?"

"The police are wondering if he shot Loretta and then killed himself," Colton told her.

"I don't know what to say. I would love not to be their prime suspect, but I can't imagine that Frank did this either. I mean, we went there to find out if he had any idea of who might have a reason to kill Loretta. We didn't go there because we thought he was guilty of it."

"I agree."

"What explanation did you tell the police about why you were there at Frank's house?"

"I was honest. I told them that I knew you. I told them that I couldn't believe you would do something like this, and I wanted to check things out myself, on my own dime."

"What did they say?"

"Not much. As long as I stay out of their way, what can they say?"

Sarah frowned. "Colton, can I see your phone?"

"Sure. Why?" He pulled it from his pocket and handed it to her.

"I remembered an email Loretta sent me. She liked to send a lot of emails, reminding me about various things. Normally, they drove me crazy. But while I was at the art show that night, she sent me one that I didn't even read. I told myself I would do it later, but then everything happened."

"And you wonder if she said something?"

"Yes, I do."

"See what you can find out."

She tapped several things into the phone before leaning back. "Here it is."

"What exactly did she say?"

"Sarah, I need you to take Buzz away for me for the weekend. I've left some money out for you. Please come home soon. I'll be waiting up." Sarah glanced at him. "She knew, Colton. Loretta had known something was wrong, and she was trying to protect us. But why?"

"If I had that answer, all of this would be over right now."

"You're right." Sarah frowned again. "Colton, there's something else. I know it's not as important, but—"

His back muscles tensed at the worry in her voice. "What is it, Sarah?"

"I went out to use the computer at the hotel. It's the only reason I saw that guy coming. So maybe it was stupid or maybe it saved my life."

Colton would reserve his judgment on that. All he'd asked Sarah to do was to remain in the room. Yet he couldn't argue with the point that Sarah may not have seen the man if she hadn't gone out. It didn't matter now.

"Okay…" he started.

"I got an email from the storage facility where I keep my things. It flooded and everything might be ruined."

"I'm sorry, Sarah."

"My…my paintings are all there, Colton. I know it's minor in comparison to what's going on now. But…"

"You want to go check them out?"

"Only if we can."

"I know your paintings are important to you."

"They're my life's work. I know I haven't made it big yet—maybe I never will, but—"

"You have a lot of talent, Sarah."

Her cheeks reddened. "Thank you."

"I mean it. You've always been talented. You'll have your big break one day." Colton had seen her talent from the moment he'd looked at her first painting. She had a knack for picking up on the beauty in life. For sensing things that others didn't. She was truly gifted.

"I appreciate that. I've always appreciated how much you believe in me."

"I never stopped believing in you."

At his words, he glanced at Sarah and saw her cheeks redden. He didn't want his statement to be true. He wanted to put his relationship with Sarah behind him. But he couldn't do that until he knew she was safe.

Twenty minutes later, Colton pulled up to the storage area. He hadn't been followed. But the man in the sedan had figured out a way to track them somehow earlier. Colton needed to make sure there were no other surprises.

He paused only for a moment to glance at the facility. It had interior doors, but the business was located in a bad section of town. No doubt, things had been cheaper here.

Sarah had definitely gone through some financial struggles. His heart went out to her.

Hopefully they could get some answers now, and she'd feel better.

"Let's go check it out. And then we need to hit the road again and figure out our next step, okay?"

Sarah nodded. "Okay. Let's do this."

Sarah typed in a code outside the main doors, and they hurried inside an unmanned lobby. Wasting no time, they turned left. Colton followed her down a dim hallway, pausing as she stopped by a door labeled 138.

She typed in another code on a keypad above the handle,

heard a click and shoved the door open. After flipping on the lights, they stepped inside.

Several storage rolls where her canvases were stored rested on the floor. A few mounted paintings leaned against a wall. A couple miscellaneous boxes sat in the center of the room.

"Funny, it doesn't look flooded, does it?" Sarah put her hands on her hips and glanced around, a wrinkle forming between her eyes.

Colton eyed the space, looking for any signs of moisture. Smelling for the scent of mildew. Looking for any indications there had been an incident here at the facility.

There was nothing.

"No, it doesn't look flooded," he finally said. "Unless the water has already dried up. Check your paintings. See if they're damaged."

Sarah reached down and pulled a painting from one of the lower shelves there. A picture of a waterfall stared back at them.

A flawless picture.

With no water damage.

A bright smile crossed Sarah's face. "It wasn't as bad as I thought. Maybe this area was spared."

"That would be great. Good news, right?" Colton said.

"Fantastic news."

Colton reached on top of a box and pulled something off. He seemed to operate on autopilot, not meaning to be nosy. But he couldn't stop himself.

"Is this the blanket I gave you?" he asked.

Her cheeks flushed. "Yes, it is. It's a great blanket."

Colton smiled. "Yeah, it is."

He'd had it made for her out of T-shirts they'd purchased at various state parks they'd visited. Sarah had loved it when Colton had given it to her on her twenty-fifth birthday.

But he'd just assumed Sarah had gotten rid of everything when they'd broken up.

She looked up, something strange in her gaze, like she wanted to explain herself but couldn't bring herself to do so.

Colton was just about to say something—he wasn't sure what—when he heard something slam behind him. He rushed to the door and pushed on it.

It was locked or jammed somehow.

Colton rattled it again, but nothing happened. His internal alarms began to sound.

"What?" Sarah joined him by the door and pressed on it.

It was no use. Whoever had locked them in had blocked the door too.

Buzz gave out a bark to let them know he wasn't happy.

"What's going on, Colton?" Sarah's frightened eyes met his.

"I have a feeling we were lured here." Colton hadn't wanted to say the words aloud, but it was the only thing that made sense. This had all been a trap.

Colton should have seen through it. He'd chide himself for it later.

Before he could think about his mistake anymore, he froze.

A strange smell teased his senses.

Then he realized what it was.

Gas. Someone was feeding some type of gas through a line at the bottom of the door. Gas that would most likely make them pass out soon.

"Sarah, we've got to find a way out of here," Colton said, his gaze locking with hers. "Now."

FOURTEEN

Sarah rammed her shoulder into the door. Logically, she knew if Colton couldn't break through, she couldn't either. But she didn't care right now. Panic surged through her as survival instinct took over.

That same man who'd killed Loretta was now trying to kill her, Colton and Buzz also.

She pounded on the door, desperation taking over. "Help!"

"Save your breath and stay low." After stuffing a blanket under the door, Colton took Sarah's elbow and swiftly led her to the other side of the room. "Actually, put your shirt over your mouth. I don't know what this is, but don't breathe it."

What were they going to do? There was nowhere else to go. But if they stayed in here, then they had only seconds to remain lucid.

Buzz began barking at them.

"What is it, Buzz?" Sarah asked, her head starting to swim. "I know. We're in trouble."

The dog kept barking, the sound becoming more frantic.

"I think he's trying to tell us something." Colton rushed toward Buzz. "What is it?"

The husky nuzzled his way between some boxes and

continued barking at something in the corner. Colton pushed boxes aside and followed behind him.

"Sarah, it's a vent," Colton muttered.

She knelt beside him, her eyes widening when she saw the larger-than-average opening. "Look at that! Can we get through it?"

"We don't have any other choice but to try." He pulled out a pocketknife and began to work the edges of the grate. Finally, the top released and Colton pulled the metal cover off.

Sarah knelt down lower on the ground, coughing with every other breath. The gas was getting thicker, becoming harder to avoid.

If they didn't get out soon, they wouldn't leave here alive. She felt certain.

Colton tossed the vent cover behind him and stuck his head into the space. "It's narrow, but if you head right and then follow it, we should be able to escape. I'm going to let Buzz go first then you. You can do this, okay?"

Sarah nodded, even though she felt anything but confident. What other choice did they have? None.

Buzz barked once more before climbing in through the fifteen by fifteen opening and leading the way. Saying a quick prayer, Sarah climbed in behind him.

The gas had started to fill this area, as well. She pulled her shirt up higher over her mouth and nose, trying to protect her lungs for as long as possible.

"You're doing great," Colton said behind her.

She didn't feel great. She felt claustrophobic. The space was so dark, and her limbs were getting heavy. The sound of Buzz's claws on metal made her skin crawl.

The dog seemed to instinctively know where they were going. As quickly as she could, Sarah followed behind him. Her knees ached from moving in the cramped space. Her palms were sore. But she kept moving.

They reached the end of the tunnel, and another surge of panic went through her.

What now? Where would they go? Had they come this far just to perish?

Buzz pawed at something.

"Is that another vent?" Colton murmured.

She tried to peer around Buzz. "It's another vent cover."

"Can you push it out?" Colton asked.

"Let me see." She squeezed her arm around Buzz and shoved the cover.

Nothing.

Shoved it harder.

Still nothing.

Giving it one last burst of energy, she pushed against it one last time.

Finally, the metal cover clattered to the ground. Buzz jumped out onto the vinyl floor below.

Sarah pushed herself to make it the last few feet. She climbed from the opening and nearly collapsed on the floor.

But she didn't have time to gather herself. Instead, she glanced around. They were in a stairwell, she realized.

Colton climbed out behind Sarah and took her hand. "Come on. We've got to get out of here."

Sarah didn't have time to think. To breathe.

They left the building, sprinted back to his truck and jumped inside before whomever it was who'd lured them here caught them.

As darkness fell around them, Colton stared at the lonely mountain road. A stretch of blacktop snaked across the mountainside, barely visible except for where his headlights shone. The area was still, as was the conversation inside his truck.

Both of them seemed to be lost in their own thoughts.

The effects of the gas had worn off as soon as they'd stopped breathing it in.

Gas.

That man hadn't wanted to kill them. He'd wanted to knock them out, hadn't he? Why was that? What was the man's endgame?

Colton couldn't figure it out. He only knew that had been incredibly close, and this situation could have turned out so much differently.

His phone buzzed. As he pulled to a stop, he glanced at the screen and sucked in a breath.

"What is it?" Sarah asked.

He hesitated a moment before showing her the screen. "I'm sorry, Sarah."

The pictures showed Sarah's paintings from the storage area. They'd been ripped apart.

She let out a gasp. "No..."

"We must have ticked this guy off when we escaped. I'm so sorry."

"And now he must know who you are," Sarah said. "He texted these pictures to you."

"He probably traced my license plates or something."

Beside him, Sarah said nothing. She only stared out the window, appearing shell-shocked and in mourning.

Yet again.

So many losses and tragedies, and now her paintings.

Colton's heart went out to her. He knew Sarah had lost years of work, and he couldn't imagine how that might feel.

But right now, they didn't talk. Colton knew Sarah well enough to know that she needed time to process—and that's what she was doing right now. There would be time to talk later.

Thirty minutes after that, he pulled to a stop in front of an old log cabin on the edge of the Idaho line. The windows were dark, and snow covered the roof of the tiny nine-hundred-square-foot place. Colton hadn't been here in years.

"Where are we?" Sarah asked, a knot forming between her eyes as she stared at the dark house.

"It's a cabin an old friend of mine owns," he told her. "He said I could use it whenever I want. Turns out, I need it now."

Sarah nodded slowly before reaching down to grab her purse. "Perfect."

Colton's boots hit the ground. He walked around to the other side of the truck and helped Sarah out. Buzz followed behind them.

The snow crunched beneath their feet as they tromped to the front door. Colton reached below a rock on the steps and retrieved the key.

A moment later, they were inside. The place smelled dusty, like it had been closed up too long. But it was safe.

For now.

As Sarah stood there shivering in the middle of the room, Colton walked to the fireplace. Wood had been left there.

He quickly grabbed some logs and put them in the brick enclosure. In a basket on the hearth, he found a lighter and began to work on getting some flames started.

"Listen, can you check the kitchen?" Colton asked Sarah over his shoulder. "See if there's anything to eat. Maybe some canned soup that's not expired or something. My friend usually leaves the electric on here so the pipes won't freeze. Winter is his favorite time to come here normally, but I happen to know he's in Wyoming on a hunting trip right now."

"Of course I'll check." Sarah walked into the kitchen and began opening cabinets.

It would be good for her to have something to do, to keep her mind occupied.

A few minutes later, soup simmered on the stove, and a fire blazed. Colton had apparently turned up the heat, as well, because the whole place felt warmer.

Sarah ladled the beef stew into coffee mugs for her and Colton and put some dog food in a bowl for Buzz. They then sat on the hearth to eat. The heat warmed their skin and began thawing them out.

Colton watched the dog eat for a moment, marveling at how well behaved he was. "What happens to Buzz after this?"

Sarah put her spoon back into her mug. "I don't know. There's no one else to take him. But if I'm in jail…"

"You won't be." Colton paused. "I'm sorry about your paintings, Sarah. I would have saved them if I could."

She nodded slowly, her lips pulling down in a slight frown and a new sadness filling her gaze. "I know you would have. Do you think they're all destroyed?"

Colton didn't know what to say. Instead, he shrugged and put his spoon back into his mug. "I want to tell you no, but I… I can't do that. Who knows what this guy is up to?"

"This is all a disaster, Colton. Everything. My life. I guess it's following a pattern."

"Your life hasn't been a disaster, Sarah."

"Yes, it has been. From my dad leaving, my mom going to prison and then dying, going into foster care. Every time I make plans, they don't work out. Maybe that's why it's better if I don't make plans."

Was that one of the reasons she'd left him? Colton wasn't sure, but he would guess the answer to be yes.

"Life doesn't work out the way we want it to. But sometimes, life can be beautiful. You have to take the good with the bad. Be willing to be flexible. Accept that there's beauty with pain."

She looked at him, a new emotion glimmering in her eyes. "I'm glad you're doing better, Colton."

He set his empty mug on the table. "I went through a hard time after I shot that man, Sarah."

"A hard time? You changed your whole life. Instead of wanting to stay in Seattle, you decided to move to the mountains of Idaho and give up your job."

Colton shrugged. "Maybe it had been coming for a while. Everything had been building up. I'm not sure I ever intended on staying in Seattle long-term."

"What do you mean?"

"I don't know. I've never enjoyed the pressure of the city. The busyness of the rat race. The tension of always feeling pressure to perform. I just didn't want to spend my entire future like that. Especially not if I had kids. I wanted them to feel like they could breathe and explore and be content with the quiet."

Curiosity sparked in her gaze. "You didn't feel like you could breathe?"

"No, I felt like I was suffocating." He glanced up at her. "I hoped you could see the possibilities in moving also. In fact, I thought you would love the idea, that we'd be on the same page."

"It's hard to have a career in art when you're hundreds of miles from everything."

"Or it could have been inspiration." Colton stopped himself and shook his head. "It doesn't matter now, does it?"

Sarah frowned. "No, it doesn't."

Colton stood. "Look, maybe we should get some rest. Tomorrow we need to keep looking for answers. We're going to need our energy if we do that."

Sarah nodded again, but she opened her mouth, like she wanted to talk more.

"We'll be safe here—for the night, at least," Colton continued. He stood and handed her a blanket from the back of the couch. "Besides, Buzz will keep an eye on things for us. He saved us today."

Sarah reached over and patted the dog's head. "He sure did. Twice."

As she bedded down on the couch, Buzz lay on the floor beneath her, the ever-vigilant guard dog.

That was good—because they needed all the protection they could get right now. Not just physically.

Sarah reminded herself to protect her heart, as well.

FIFTEEN

Sarah swallowed a scream as she pulled her eyes open.

The masked man. Where was he?

Her heart pounded out of control as her gaze swung around the room.

"Sarah, it's just a dream."

A tremble raked through her. It really had been a dream. A nightmare.

The masked man wasn't here. No, Colton was here, and he was watching over her, as was Buzz.

She let out a moan as the memories hit her.

This wasn't all a bad dream. No, she was in a desperate situation that she might never recover from.

She blinked. The fire blazed behind her, adding warmth to the room. Buzz lay on the floor beside her place on the couch, looking rather content considering the situation.

Colton came into view. He sat beside her, staring at her with concern in his gaze.

"You okay?" he asked. "That must have been some dream."

"Yeah, it really was." She ran a hand through her hair, trying to gain control of her racing heart.

She'd slept surprisingly hard and needed to gather her

wits. But as she saw Colton's phone appear, she noticed that he was staring at it, a concerned expression on his face.

"What's going on?" Sarah pulled the blanket up higher, trying to ward away the cold chill in the air. Based on the wet footprints on the floor, Colton had taken Buzz outside. Opening the door must have added a burst of cold to the room.

Colton said nothing for a minute, almost as if he didn't want to say anything. Instead, he stood, grabbed a coffee mug, and poured some warm liquid into the cup.

He walked over and handed it to her. "Sorry, no cream."

"That's okay." She let the heat from the ceramic mug warm her fingers, feeling incredibly grateful for Colton's kindness. "Thank you."

"No problem." He stiffly sat across from her.

Something was up. What wasn't he telling her? Sarah knew him better than the average person and could tell when he had something on his mind.

"What's going on, Colton?" she asked again.

After a moment of hesitation, he picked up his phone and showed her his screen. "There's security footage of you going into the storage facility yesterday."

"What?" Alarm stiffened her muscles.

He nodded. "The police think you were trying to destroy evidence that might implicate you in Loretta's murder."

"I would never…"

His level gaze met hers. "I know that, Sarah. But, on paper—or film, I should say—it looks bad."

Another thought hit Sarah and sent a fresh round of worry through her system. "What about you? Did the security camera pick you up also?"

"You can see me, but you can't make out my features."

Well, that was good…maybe. "What about the parking lot? Did they get your license plate?"

"If they have, they haven't released that information."

"This is bad, Colton." She pulled the blanket up higher around her, finding tactile comfort in the action.

He nodded. "I know."

"I didn't mean to pull you into this." She couldn't say that enough.

"Someone is trying their best to implicate you, Sarah. This isn't your fault."

"I know. But your career..." He'd worked so hard at his job—a job where reputation was everything. He couldn't lose it all because of her.

"There are things more important than a career."

Colton's words sent a wave of warmth through her. He meant that, didn't he? Sarah had been running scared, so afraid of getting close to someone, only to be hurt again. But what if that wasn't the case when it came to Colton?

She'd have to think about that later, when there weren't so many other pressing concerns around her.

"What about Frank?" she asked, pulling her legs beneath her. "Any updates?"

"Unfortunately, a neighbor said he saw you at Frank's house yesterday." Colton frowned as he said the words, like he didn't want to say them but had no other choice.

Despair tried to bite deep. "I just can't catch a break. It's like everything's working against me."

Colton moved until he was beside her on the couch, close enough that she could feel the warmth of his body heat as their legs touched.

She brushed off the rush of electricity she felt.

"The police have their blinders on," Colton said.

"What am I going to do?"

"I want to have a conversation with Loretta's lawyer," Colton said. "I want to get his thoughts on the situation. Did he work for her company or for Loretta personally?"

"My impression is that Alfred Jennings worked for Loretta, doing more personal things like wills and things of that nature." Sarah shifted. "What about Yvonne—the head of the other company that's competition? We could talk to her."

"She's on my list also, but she's been out of the country. She still is—at least according to social media. She's been posting pictures of herself in Africa. I checked this morning."

Sarah frowned and leaned back. "So what do we do?"

"We need more information if we're going to find answers. I believe someone not only wants something from you, but also views you as a threat. We need to figure out why."

"I'll do whatever it takes."

Colton stood. "Great. Why don't you get cleaned up? We're going back into town to pay a visit to Alfred Jennings. I want to know what he knows. But we're going to have to be very, very careful."

Sarah swallowed hard, unsure if she was ready for this or not. Because careful might not keep her alive. But finding answers was going to require risk. She couldn't ask Colton to put his life on the line while she sought safety.

But she'd never been so scared in her life.

Sarah's lungs became tighter and tighter with every minute they got closer to the law offices of Jennings, Morrow and Smith. As they pulled to a stop in front of the large building located on the outskirts of town, she felt beside herself and could hardly breathe.

She'd gotten Colton into this mess, and she couldn't let him take the fall for her. No, she wanted to be there when he talked to Alfred Jennings. She couldn't send Colton onto the battlefield alone. It wasn't right.

"I need to talk to Jennings, Colton," Sarah announced, resolve solidifying inside her.

Colton glanced at her. "I don't think that's a good idea. Your face is all over the news."

She knew what the consequences would be—for both of them. And if the police came after Colton, she fully intended on telling them this was all her doing and that she'd coerced him in some way to participate.

"This is my mess," she told him. "I want to be a part of this."

"Sarah, Jennings could call the police. This could be like walking into the police station and it will undoubtedly get you arrested."

Sarah's stomach squeezed at hearing the words out loud. But she couldn't back down. "I know. But I don't want to sit in the car with Buzz. I'm no safer being away from you while you're doing these investigations than I am being with you."

Colton's jaw tensed, and he said nothing for a minute. Finally, he shrugged. "It's your choice. I advise against it, but I can't stop you."

Sarah released her breath. "Thanks. I'm going."

Colton glanced into the backseat. "What about Buzz?"

"I was thinking he could wait in the truck."

"While we go into the office building?"

"Actually, Loretta told me that Jennings has a hot dog every day for lunch from his favorite stand outside the building. Regardless of the weather, his health, anything. He's a creature of habit." She glanced at her watch. "We should be able to catch him there. If we park close enough, we can keep an eye on Buzz also."

"It sounds like a plan."

As Colton looked for a parking space, Sarah borrowed his phone and looked up Alfred Jennings's picture. She found it easily and studied the image of the man. He appeared to be in his late sixties. He had reddish-brown hair, ruddy skin, and he looked about twenty pounds overweight.

Colton parallel parked in front of the building. "You stay here, boy. Okay?"

Buzz whined.

Colton cracked his window and glanced at Sarah. "You sure you're good with this? It's not too late to change your mind."

"Yeah, I'm sure." She wasn't positive where her courage came from. But she was determined to be an active part of this investigation. Colton wasn't going to be out here alone anymore. She nodded toward the distance. "There he is."

Colton followed her gaze until it stopped on Alfred Jennings. Just as Loretta had said, the man stood beside a hot dog stand and pulled some money from his wallet before being handed his lunch, wrapped in aluminum foil.

He took his food and walked toward a park bench in front of the office building. The space contained various benches with a statue at the center. Several people, despite the bitter cold, were outside there, getting some fresh air.

The good news was that Sarah hadn't seen anyone following them yet. Maybe now that they'd gotten rid of Buzz's collar, they'd lost the man on their trail. She hoped the man pursuing them didn't have any other tricks up his sleeve—but she wouldn't put it past him, either.

"I say now is as good a time as any to talk to him," Colton said. "Keep your hat and sunglasses on. It will buy us some time."

"Whatever you say."

They climbed from Colton's truck and hurried across the sidewalk. Jennings sat with his back toward them, unaware of their presence. He looked like the picture Sarah had seen, except right now he wore a rimmed black hat, a heavy wool coat and a thick plaid scarf.

The garb seemed appropriate for such a gray, bleak day. If Sarah had to guess, they would get more snow later. The sky looked full and ready to burst with icy goodness.

Colton motioned for Sarah to stay behind him as he slid onto the bench next to Alfred. "Mr. Jennings, I was hoping you might answer some questions for me."

Jennings's eyes widened, and he stopped with his hot dog raised in the air. "Who are you?"

"I'm an investigator who's looking into Loretta Blanchard's murder."

"Do you have an ID?"

"I'm working as a consultant, but I was a detective in Seattle before coming here."

Jennings's gaze narrowed, making it clear he was still on guard. "What do you need to know?"

"I'm trying to figure out who might have killed her."

"The police have already named a suspect." He took another bite of his hot dog, not appearing shaken by Colton's questions and showing that he was a seasoned lawyer.

As they spoke, Sarah remained a safe distance away, her back toward them. Hopefully, she looked like someone who was lingering close. But she remained far enough away that Jennings might not notice her.

She glanced around, looking again for any sign of trouble or danger. The sidewalks were busy with people, but no one who stood out to her. Everyone seemed to be minding their own business. Buzz remained in the truck, the top of his head revealed through the cracked window.

Normal.

Everything appeared normal, and her danger radar indicated they were safe—for now.

Even better, Jennings didn't seem to notice that Sarah

was there. Instead, he mostly focused on his hot dog and Colton.

Good. That bought them some time. At present.

Just as Colton was about to ask another question, Jennings continued.

"I don't know what I can tell you," Jennings said. "Loretta was a good woman. She didn't deserve to die like that. But I have no idea who might have done it other than that new assistant of hers."

His words hit Sarah. She was the scapegoat here—and an easy one, at that.

How would she ever convince anyone that she hadn't done this?

SIXTEEN

"You think her assistant did this?" Colton glanced back at Sarah as she lingered a few steps away, but close enough to listen. This couldn't be easy for her to hear.

Jennings's expression softened. "I don't want to believe it."

"Why not?"

"Loretta really liked that girl. Said she saw some of herself in her."

"But her assistant was an artist, not a scientist." Colton had no choice but to act like the bad guy for a moment.

Jennings shrugged. "I think it was the passion for her work that she related to. Loretta said Sarah was a wonderful artist and that she wanted to help her out. Honestly, I think she saw the same loneliness in Sarah that she felt herself. Loretta was pretty much all by herself in this world. Just like Sarah."

Colton's heart thudded in his chest at the thought of it. "Is that right?"

"I honestly don't believe the girl did it. I don't know what happened, but I don't believe Loretta's assistant is the culprit. I've never met her before, but Loretta had a good instinct about her."

That was a great first step to having this conversation.

"The drug business is cutthroat. Was there anyone Loretta had problems with?"

Jennings sighed and discarded the rest of his hot dog into a nearby trash can. "I don't know. I can say that Loretta wasn't acting like herself the few days before she died. I thought maybe it was her ALS. But she didn't tell me anything."

"And you don't have any theories?" Colton continued, feeling like the man might still know more than he let on.

Jennings frowned and looked up at Colton. "This is the only thing I can think to tell you. Loretta was on the verge of creating a drug that would help people with ALS. That has been her goal for the past several years."

Colton sucked in a breath. Could it be the lead they'd been looking for? "Did she tell many people about it?"

"No. Loretta was working on it on her own. She had a lab there at the company where she could work privately. It was one of the perks of starting her own business, I suppose. She didn't want to tell anyone more than necessary. She did have some control groups, but they'd signed confidentiality clauses so they couldn't tell others."

Colton crossed his arms, trying to think that through. "Is that even legal?"

"I drew up the contract myself. I made sure she was covered. The people involved had seen significant results."

"All of them?" Colton asked, his interest piqued. Because, if not, they might have a new pool of suspects.

"Yes," Jennings said. "From what I understood, they'd all had good results. I can't imagine any of them wanting to hurt her."

"Was there anyone who wanted to get into the program but couldn't? That would be a reason to have a grudge against her."

Jennings shrugged. "Again, because of the confidentiality of it all, I can't see that happening."

"Last question—was there anyone helping her with this? Anyone on her staff who knew what she was doing?"

"From what she told me, no. She only told me because she had to. Otherwise, she kept quiet. She learned her lesson when she split with her friend Yvonne, and Yvonne started her own company. She vowed she wouldn't make that mistake again."

"So it sounds like Yvonne was an enemy." Colton scanned the crowds one more time but didn't see anyone who grabbed his attention. Good. But he still couldn't let down his guard.

"They had a professional competitiveness about them, but I do believe that Loretta ultimately respected the woman's work."

Just then, Colton did a double take. Buzz had somehow managed to jump out of the truck window. The dog bounded toward them, looking like he was on a mission.

Colton looked back at Sarah and saw her eyes widen, as well.

Jennings looked twice when he spotted Buzz. "Wait… is that…?"

Colton looked back at Sarah once more, just in time to see a man appear from nowhere and sprint toward her.

"No!" he yelled.

Colton lunged toward Sarah. But the man reached her before Colton did.

The man grabbed her arm, tackling her to the ground.

Around them, people began to scatter. A few screamed. Several stopped to stare.

Colton glanced over as a streak of fur went past him. Buzz.

The dog darted past Colton, his teeth bared.

He growled before springing on the man. He knocked him off-balance, but the man quickly pulled himself to his feet.

The next instant, the attacker turned on his heel and took off.

Sarah lay on the ground, rubbing her elbow and looking shaken.

Buzz stood guard beside her.

Colton knelt beside Sarah. "Are you okay?"

She looked up, dazed. "Yeah, but we need to get out of here."

"Yes, we do." Colton helped her to her feet.

As he did, he glanced back at Jennings. Concern stretched across the man's face, along with the realization that Sarah was here…and in trouble.

"Good luck," the man muttered, a flash of compassion in his eyes. "Figure out who did this."

Colton wasted no more time. They had to leave this place. Now.

With Sarah's hand in his, they ran toward his truck and climbed inside with Buzz. As soon as the keys were in the ignition, they took off, trying to get as far away from the scene as possible.

"What just happened?" Sarah asked, holding on to the door handle, her breaths coming rapidly.

"I'm still not sure. What was in your purse?"

She shrugged. "Nothing. I mean, nothing of value."

"Nothing from Loretta?" Colton asked, trying to put the pieces together. He headed out of town, going fast—but not fast enough to be noticed.

"No, nothing. There was ChapStick and my wallet. Nothing else."

Colton frowned and wove into the left lane. As he stared

straight ahead at the road, the first snowflakes began hitting his windshield.

"That man wants something badly, Sarah," he said. "He'll do anything to get it. He took a big risk by doing that out in public."

"Exactly. But why would he do that?" She took her hat off and raked a hand through her hair. "It just doesn't make sense."

"I have no idea." Colton didn't like any of this. He could feel danger squeezing tighter.

Sarah stared straight ahead, the snow seeming to transfix her for a moment. Then she leaned back, crossed her arms and let out a long breath. "What are we doing now?"

"We need to get far away from here before the police come."

"They'll be looking for your truck."

"You're probably right. But we're going to have to take that chance right now. We don't have any time to waste."

Sarah glanced at Colton, curiosity—and maybe fear—entering her voice. "What are you thinking?"

"I'm thinking that I want to take a look at Loretta's house."

Sarah sucked in a breath. "Why in the world would you want to do that? The police probably have eyes on the place."

"Actually, I doubt they do. They probably don't think you'll come back—not with your face all over the news."

"But why chance it?"

Colton swallowed hard, the plan solidifying in his mind. "Because I need to see it. I need to see if there's anything the police missed. I need to know if anything at the house is different now than when you left."

"What if we're caught?"

"We'll be careful."

She slunk down lower in the seat. "I don't know if I like this, Colton."

He frowned, totally understanding where she was coming from and empathizing. "I don't either. But we don't have any other choice right now. But first, before we go there, maybe we should grab a bite to eat. How does that sound?"

"Great."

Good. He needed to collect his thoughts. Because this mystery was feeling more and more complicated—and dangerous—by the moment.

Sarah breathed easier as they pulled out of town and onto some back roads. She had so much to think about. To process. To attempt to comprehend.

Colton pulled up to a gas station with a fast food restaurant inside. He chose a spot to the side of the building, out of sight to anyone driving past, and put his truck into Park.

"How about if I run inside and grab some food?" he asked. "I can bring it out to the truck to eat, we'll get gas, walk Buzz and give him some water. It will be a nice breather for all of us."

"Sounds like a plan. If they have a grilled chicken sandwich, that would be perfect. Maybe with a side of salad or fruit."

"That's what I was going to guess." As Colton climbed out, he offered a smile that sent flutters through Sarah.

"And grab a new collar for Buzz if you could," she called.

"Of course."

It had only been two years since they were together, so it probably shouldn't be surprising that he remembered so much. Yet a small part of her still felt delight in knowing he hadn't forgotten what she liked.

Did he think about her as much as Sarah thought about him?

It wasn't important. It was all water under the bridge. There were trust issues between them—issues she wasn't sure they could get past. Sometimes desire wasn't enough to change the facts, and it definitely wasn't enough to change history.

She glanced around, looking for any signs of trouble. She saw nothing but trucks full of people headed out for outdoor adventures. No one looked their way, and Sarah hoped it would stay like that.

As a moment of silence fell, Sarah reflected on Loretta's words. The woman really had liked her. More than liked her. She must have thought of her as a daughter almost.

How could Sarah not have known that?

Despite the hurt and pang of loss, a surge of satisfaction welled up in her. Loretta really had seen something in Sarah. The news caused a warm delight to spread through her.

Several minutes later, Colton climbed back inside with two bags of food, two cups of coffee and a large cup of water. He handed Sarah one of the sacks.

She opened her bag, and her stomach grumbled at the scent of grilled chicken. She hadn't realized how hungry she was.

"They had chicken," Colton said.

"Perfect."

He opened the cup of water and put it in the backseat for Buzz. The dog gulped it up, obviously thirsty from their adventures today.

As they all settled back with their food, Colton cleared

his throat. "So, how did you know where to find me? I didn't realize you knew where my cabin was."

Sarah shrugged, picked a pickle from her sandwich before it fell off and popped it in her mouth. "Your mom told me."

"My mom?" Colton's eyes widened as he glanced at her, as if he hadn't heard correctly.

Sarah smiled at his shock. She'd wondered if he knew about those letters and had assumed that he didn't. "She liked to write me letters. You didn't know?"

"I had no idea." He wiped his mouth with a napkin.

"Yes, she kept me updated. Told me where you'd moved. Even sent me your address in case I ever wanted to visit. I kept some of those letters in my glove compartment, so I was able to find your address when I left with Buzz that night. I drove around for hours, unsure where to go or what to do. And then… I did the only thing that made sense."

"You came to my place."

Sarah nodded. "I went to your place."

He didn't say anything for a moment until finally shaking his head. "My mom… I can't believe she did that. I don't even know what to say."

"She sent me letters more often right after we broke up. Told me how much she missed me. Asked me to change my mind and come back."

Colton lowered his burger and let out a long puff of air. "I'm so sorry, Sarah. She's a meddler for sure, but I didn't know…"

"It's okay. Actually, you know how much I loved your family. It was nice to stay connected. And she was always kind to me—even in the letters. She didn't push me as much as she let me know how much I was missed. It's good to feel missed."

A moment of silence stretched between them. "Did she

tell you that she and my father are down in Arizona during the winter?"

"She did. She sounds like she likes it in that area." Mama Hawk, as she was called, had told Sarah all about her adventures in retirement. The art of letter writing was becoming lost, but Colton's mom had perfected it. Sarah loved those letters.

"Yeah, I think she does."

Sarah finished her sandwich and turned to Colton, still sensing he was uneasy about his mom's involvement in Sarah's life over the past two years. "You know, Colton, you're really blessed to have parents like you do."

A sad smile crossed his face. "I know I am. I don't always agree with my mom's methods, but she's always been there for me and I know she loves me. She took our breakup really hard. Maybe even harder than I realized."

"Bringing someone into your family and then losing them…it's hard." The words caught in her throat. Sarah had been through so many foster families after her mom had gone to jail. The hardest part was feeling a connection with someone who would take her in, only to have that family send her away for various reasons. It had always felt like her fault, even when it wasn't.

And then there was the fact that she and her sister had been separated. Though they both still kept in touch, something had changed between them during their time apart. Their relationship had never been the same.

"I guess you know all about that." Colton's soft voice indicated that he understood, that he felt compassion.

Sarah glanced at her hands. "Yeah, unfortunately, I do."

"Do you ever wonder what our lives would be like now if we hadn't broken up?"

Every day. Sarah swallowed the words, though. "It doesn't matter, does it? We can't change the past."

"No, we can't." Colton's words sounded as strained as her heart felt.

But it was true. The past was behind them—all their mistakes. And sometimes, you couldn't fix things. You just had to move forward.

Even though this highly charged situation might make Sarah feel like the two of them had a chance together, she had to remember that facing danger together wasn't the same as being in a relationship.

Right now, she just had to concentrate on staying alive.

SEVENTEEN

Sarah could hardly breathe as they pulled up to Loretta's house an hour later. Just seeing the huge, six-thousand-square-foot house brought a rush of memories. It was a grand house, framed out in brick with no expense spared.

The lots in this neighborhood were large—about three or four acres each. Woods came up to the back of the property, along with a stunning skyline.

Flashes of seeing that man standing over Loretta filled her mind. Of Buzz knocking the killer off Loretta. Of running for her life.

A tremble raked through her body.

Buzz nuzzled her face, seeming to sense her thoughts—or maybe the dog was feeling the same way. Canines grieved also. Certainly Buzz missed Loretta right now.

As Colton drove around to the back of the secluded residence, Sarah didn't spot any other cars there. Good. At least this part of the plan was going smoothly. Colton parked behind the garage.

Before opening his door, Colton turned toward Sarah, concern in his gaze. The way he still respected her despite their history touched Sarah and made her crave the happy times of their past.

Back then, Colton would have done anything for her, just like he was doing now.

She'd forgotten how good it felt to have someone like that in her life. A jolt of sadness sliced through the tension she felt inside.

"Are you ready for this, Sarah?" Colton asked, his gaze searching hers—probably looking for the truth despite her bravado.

She shrugged, knowing there was no need to deny reality. "As ready as I'll ever be, I guess."

With one last glance at her, Colton nodded and looked toward the stately house in the distance. "Okay. Let's go inside. But be careful. I don't want to draw any attention or compromise the scene. Okay?"

She nodded. "Okay."

Buzz followed behind them as they darted toward the back door. He trotted, a new bounce in his step. Did he expect to see Loretta?

More sadness pressed on Sarah.

"You still have your key?" Colton asked, his arm brushing Sarah's and sending a shiver through her.

Something about his voice sent another jolt of awareness through her. He was using that tone with her—a personal one. Earlier, he'd only sounded professional and aloof, merely acquainted. She wasn't sure what had changed, but she felt something unseen connecting them at the moment.

Sarah snapped back to reality and pulled the keys from her purse. With shaky hands, she unlocked the back door, memories flashing through her mind of the last time she'd done that—when she'd returned here absolutely clueless about what she would find inside. About Buzz being in her closet. A man being in Loretta's room.

She hesitated before stepping inside, staring at the interior as bad memories flooded her mind.

"I'll go first," Colton said softly. He paused in front of

her for long enough to swirl a strand of her hair and brush it between his fingers.

Their gazes caught for a moment, and Sarah's heart fluttered out of control.

She wanted nothing more than to reach up and plant a kiss on his lips. To relive old times.

But that would be a mistake. She had to keep reminding herself of that. Reminding herself that everyone she'd ever loved had left her. Her heart couldn't face that again. One more loss like that might crush her for good.

Colton leaned toward her and gently pressed a kiss on her forehead before whispering, "I've got your back. Always."

The moment ended as quickly as it had started. Colton brushed past Sarah and scanned the area before motioning for her to follow. Buzz waited behind her, silently insisting on bringing up the rear.

Sarah followed behind Colton.

It was obvious the police had been here. Smears of black fingerprint dust stained various surfaces. Drawers were open, as if they'd been searched.

Had the cops found anything?

"Where is Loretta's room?" Colton asked.

"This way." Sarah remembered the brief moment they'd shared, and her cheeks heated. But she quickly pushed those feelings aside and pointed down the first level of the west wing.

She directed Colton all the way there but paused before peering inside Loretta's room herself. She knew what she'd see in that room, and Sarah wasn't sure she was prepared to relive those moments.

Buzz remained in the hallway with her, sniffing the floor like a dog on a mission.

A moment later, Colton stepped out. "We need to figure out if anything is different here, Sarah. You're the best one to do that."

"What do you mean by anything?"

"It can be even the smallest change." He reached down and squeezed her hand. "I know it's going to be hard, but could you take a look?"

She drew in a deep, shaky breath and nodded. "Okay."

Colton didn't let go of her hand as they stepped inside— and she didn't pull away. No, she needed someone to lean on if she was going to face this crime scene again.

She paused in the room, her throat tightening as memories bombarded her. She could so clearly see Loretta sitting by the window just thinking. She did that a lot and said that's how she came up with her best ideas.

That was how Sarah often found her inspiration also.

Maybe she and Loretta weren't that different after all.

"Anything?" Colton asked.

Sarah forced herself to scan the room. Loretta's dresser looked the same. The pictures on top were still there.

The bed and sheets also looked the same.

Everything appeared just as it had been, except for the bloodstain on the floor and a missing rug that must have also had some evidence on it.

"There's nothing—" Sarah started.

But she stopped herself and pointed.

"What?" Colton asked.

"Except that." She stepped across the room toward a painting of mountains and a waterfall.

"That's one of your pieces of artwork," Colton muttered.

Sarah nodded. "It is. It's the painting Loretta bought when we met. The thing is, it used to only be a canvas. There was no frame. Now there is."

"Let's see if we can figure out why."

Colton pulled the sleeves of his Henley down over his fingers before reaching for the picture.

The painting really was gorgeous. The colors that Sarah had chosen were vibrant and pulled the viewer into the scene, making them want to dive into the picture and live there for a minute. He could see why Loretta had chosen it.

But it was strange that in the days before Loretta had died, she'd had this framed without mentioning anything to Sarah.

"You didn't notice this on the night Loretta died?" Colton asked, carefully grasping the edges of the painting.

"I didn't... I mean, I didn't look. But I was in here earlier that day, in the morning, and I think I would have noticed that." Nervous energy emanated off Sarah as she hovered beside him.

He understood—they both understood—the significance of this moment.

The painting released from the wall and Colton carefully carried it to the bed. He pulled a knife from his pocket and pried the backing away. His heart raced with anticipation.

Did this mean anything? Colton didn't know. But he definitely wanted to find out.

Sarah stepped closer to him, and her sweet smell reminded him of better times. Made him miss those moments.

This wasn't the time to think about that. No, this life-or-death situation had to take priority.

The back popped off, and Colton pulled it away. He didn't know what he expected to find. But he thought it was strange that Loretta had gone through this trouble and not mentioned anything to Sarah.

"Colton, what's that?" Sarah whispered.

Using his knife, he slid an envelope from the back of the painting. It had been taped there.

His breath hitched.

This was it, he realized.

This was the clue they'd been looking for. He felt sure of it.

The police wouldn't have noticed a painting like this. Wouldn't have thought to check behind it.

Only Sarah would have.

Which was what made it the perfect place to leave an envelope like this.

"You want to open this?" Colton asked.

Sarah's eyes were wide as she stared at it. Finally, she nodded. "Yeah, I do."

"You want to be alone?"

She shook her head. "No, would you stay with me?"

He reached down and squeezed her hand. "Of course."

Drawing in a shaky breath, Sarah took the envelope from him and carefully opened the seal. Colton braced himself for whatever they were about to learn.

Sarah could hardly see the words scrawled on the note that she slipped from the envelope. But she definitely recognized Loretta's beautiful scrawl with all of its loops and magnificence. As an artist, Sarah knew how to appreciate the simple things—even something like handwriting.

"I… I can't read it," Sarah said. "My hands are shaking too much."

"Would you like me to read it for you?" Colton asked, stepping up beside her—close enough that they touched. That she could smell his leathery scent. That she could feel the electricity between them.

"If you don't mind."

He took the paper from her and cleared his throat. "'Sarah, if you found this, it probably means something has happened to me. I know we've only known each other a short while, but I saw something in you instantly—some of the same qualities I saw in myself. Determination. Passion. And even loneliness.'"

Tears rushed to Sarah's eyes. Had it been that obvious?

"'I know my death will probably come as a shock to you and to most people. But I've felt for a while that someone was after me. I probably should have said something, but I feared it could be my disease acting up and messing with my mind.'" Colton glanced up at her. "Sarah, this note might clear you."

Her heart raced with anticipation. Maybe he was right. "Go on. Please."

"'When you're rich, you never know if people like you for who you are or for your money. But when I met you in the park, I knew you loved Buzz without ever having a clue about me or my wealth. And, if you could do that, I knew you were a good person. We need more good people in the world.'" Colton used his thumb to wipe away the moisture beneath Sarah's eye. "You are a good person, Sarah."

"How could you say that after everything we went through? I can't believe you don't hate me."

"You're not the kind of person a guy can hate. You're too kind."

His words sucked the air from her lungs. Did that mean he still cared for her? That maybe they could even like each other again and be friends?

The thought shouldn't bring her so much joy, but it did.

Colton turned back to the letter. "'When I was first starting out in this business, someone believed in me and gave me money to help get my business started. I would never be where I'm at today without that person. Sarah, I know you struggle with trying to make it in the art world. I don't have many regrets in life, but one of them is that I never married and had children. Toward the end of life, you realize how utterly alone you are in the world. It was just me and Buzz for the longest time.'"

Sarah reached down and rubbed Buzz's head. The dog leaned into her touch as he sat there beside them, acting like he understood every word Colton spoke.

"'As I've been thinking about the end of my life and the legacy I want to leave, I've decided several things. Upon my death, I want half of my money to go to the charities outlined in my will. But I want the rest to go to you, Sarah.'"

Sarah gasped. "What?"

"You had no idea she was leaving her money to you?" Colton studied her face.

"No, no idea. I've only known her a few months." Why would someone leave that much money to a virtual stranger?

"It sounds like she really believed in you."

"I had no idea."

Sarah wiped the tears that had begun to stream down her face. Loretta's words had touched her more than she'd imagined. She was still having trouble comprehending all of this.

"This could also make you even more of a suspect, Sarah." Colton's soft words felt like a lightning strike in the room.

"What?"

"It gives you a motive, Sarah."

"But she said she felt like someone was after her."

"Yeah, in the days since you moved into the house. The police will turn this around and think that you're that person."

She hung her head. "We really do need to find the person responsible, don't we?"

"Yeah, we really do."

"What do we do with the letter in the meantime?" She

looked at the words that Loretta had so carefully crafted. Words that brought her both comfort and distress.

"I'm going to hold on to it—for now. We'll return things the way we left them. We'll figure out the best course of action later."

Sarah nodded. "Okay."

As Colton put the painting back together, Sarah walked to the window. She peered out and spotted Loretta's neighbor Mr. Everett walk into the garage behind his house.

How could Sarah have forgotten about him? The man was always watching this house. Watching Loretta. It had been so strange… Sarah had thought about asking Loretta about it, but she hadn't had the chance.

But maybe today was the day she could find out some answers.

EIGHTEEN

Colton looked over at Sarah, noting the change in her demeanor just now as she looked out the window. What had she seen? Trouble? The police?

"What is it, Sarah?"

"Mr. Everett next door," Sarah said quickly, glancing back at Colton. "He was always watching everything. What if he saw something on the night of the murder?"

"It's a possibility, I suppose. I'm sure the police have already talked to him, though."

Her words rushed together as excitement lit in her eyes. "But we don't know what he told them. And his son is a cop. Maybe that's why Loretta said not to trust the police. Maybe Mr. Everett is somehow involved in this and his son is connected also."

Colton chewed on her words for a moment. She could have a point. He still found it strange that Loretta had told Sarah not to trust law enforcement. Her words had to be significant, but why?

"You sure you want to take the risk of talking to him?" Colton asked. "He could call and report you. I'm not sure the payoff will be worth it."

She grabbed his arm, her gaze filled with emotion. "I know what you're saying, but I'm desperate, Colton. I want answers. Mr. Everett could have those answers. If we catch him by surprise, we can get away before he calls the police."

Heat rushed through him as he felt her touch. Sarah had always had that effect on him, and their time apart had done nothing to change that.

He wasn't sure why he'd kissed her forehead earlier. There was just something about her vulnerability that captured his heart, that made him want to connect with her.

It was probably a mistake.

Finally, he nodded. "Then let's go see what Mr. Everett has to say."

"Thank you."

Just as carefully as they'd come into Loretta's house, they exited. Except this time, instead of heading back to the truck, they skirted around the side of the house toward the snowy hedges separating the two residences.

Colton knew this was risky, but Sarah was right. They needed answers right now.

Colton could hear classic rock blaring from a radio. Mr. Everett had his garage door open, despite the chilly weather, and he heard the sound of tools clanking inside.

"He likes to restore classic cars," Sarah whispered. "It became his new hobby after he retired as a stockbroker."

"Good to know." Colton nodded to the other side of the man's garage. "I think you and Buzz should stay out of sight. Close enough to listen, but not close enough to clue him in that you're here. Okay?"

Sarah nodded and took a step back, nudging Buzz to follow her. "Okay."

Sarah and Buzz remained behind some greenery, unable to be seen by Mr. Everett.

"Excuse me, sir," Colton started.

The man paused from examining the engine of a classic Mustang and turned down his music. "Yes?"

Colton examined the man a minute. He looked like a retired businessman with his neat white hair—still full—and lean build. His skin was relatively unwrinkled and even his work clothes looked expensive. "I'm investigating what happened to Loretta Blanchard, and I was hoping you might be able to help."

"I've already talked to the police." His voice held a sharp edge, but he didn't sound angry. No, he sounded grief stricken and cautious.

"I'm just trying to find out more information on what happened."

Mr. Everett still stared, traces of doubt in his gaze. "My son is a cop. I know how these things work."

"What department does your son work for?" Colton asked, trying to both build some comradery and find out more information.

"He's out in California now. Moved there four years ago, wanting more excitement than policing around here lent itself to."

"Everyone's looking for a little something different. I was a detective in Seattle before, and I wanted something slower paced."

"I think you're smarter than my son." Mr. Everett let out a chuckle. "Then again, I told him he should go into finance like me. My advice obviously means nothing."

"You might be surprised."

He shrugged and wiped the grease from his hands onto an old rag. "What do you want to know?"

"Did you see anything suspicious here on the night Loretta died?" Colton shifted as he waited for his answer.

"Yeah, I saw that assistant of hers and the dog run from the house like they were afraid of being caught." Mr. Everett frowned and shook his head, his shoulders slumping slightly. "It's a shame because Loretta really liked that girl. Don't want to believe she would do something like this."

Colton blanched at his incriminating words. "What about after that? Did you stick around long enough to see if anyone else came?"

"No, I called the police. I'd seen everything I needed to see."

"So you went inside to do that?"

Mr. Everett picked up his thermos and took a sip. "That's right. I didn't have my cell phone on me."

"Had you talked to Loretta's assistant before that?"

"No, but I'd seen her. She seemed nice enough. But looks can be deceiving."

The case against Sarah continued to build. And bringing her here had been the wrong choice. Colton had no doubt about that. He needed to get her out of here before Mr. Everett saw her.

But, before he could, a motorcycle heading down the road sounded in the distance. Mr. Everett stepped out to see what the commotion was.

Colton glanced at Sarah as she quickly stepped behind the building.

But it was too late.

Mr. Everett looked down and saw the dog prints in the snow.

"Who else is with you?" Mr. Everett asked, accusation flashing in his gaze. "What's your real reason for being here?"

Colton braced himself for whatever would happen next.

But he maintained his position that coming here had been a bad, bad idea.

And now all his fears might become a reality.

* * *

Sarah knew she had to step in and do something. Mr. Everett knew someone else was here. Give him a few more minutes, and he'd probably realize it was her and Buzz.

Praying she didn't regret it, she stepped out with hands raised. "It's me. Sarah Peterson and Buzz. I'm not trying to start trouble."

Mr. Everett's eyebrows shot up, and he took a step back.

"What are *you* doing here?" he gasped. "The police are looking for you. You're a murder suspect."

"I didn't kill Loretta," Sarah said. "I'm trying to find answers."

"Are you not really a cop?" Mr. Everett's gaze swerved to Colton.

"I was a detective in Seattle for eight years, but I'm on a break right now. Mr. Everett, Sarah didn't kill Loretta."

"I'll let a court decide that." Mr. Everett took another step back, like he might take off in a run to get his phone.

"Mr. Everett, please," Sarah pleaded. "Just hear me out for a moment. I'm trying to figure out what happened to Loretta. I saw a man in her room attack her before she died. Buzz jumped on him. I need to figure out who that was."

His eyes still held doubt, but he didn't look ready to do anything stupid—not for the moment, at least. Instead, he reached toward Buzz, who'd sauntered over to him, tail wagging.

"You miss her, don't you, boy?" Mr. Everett murmured. "She always said you were a special dog."

Sarah's heart warmed at the sight of Mr. Everett with Buzz. A certain amount of loss saturated his words, bent his body. If this situation was different at the moment, their grief might have bonded them all.

"How do I know you're not making all of this up?"

Mr. Everett finally asked, straightening and putting his hands on his hips.

Sarah stepped closer. "Because I cared about Loretta. Because I'm living a nightmare right now. Because I'm putting everything on the line to find answers." Sarah's voice cracked with emotion as she looked at Mr. Everett.

The man continued to stare.

"Anything you might know will help," Colton said. "Did you see anything else that night?"

"The only thing I saw was you running." Mr. Everett's gaze fell back on Sarah.

Another thought continued to nudge her. Sarah knew she was taking a risk by saying this aloud, but she had no choice. "Mr. Everett, I saw you watching Loretta on more than one occasion. Why did you always keep an eye on her?"

His face paled. "What? You don't know what you're talking about."

"I do, though," Sarah continued. "I saw you on more than one occasion. What aren't you telling us? Are *you* behind all of this?"

He gasped, his eyes turning beady. "I would never, ever hurt Loretta. Never."

"Then why were you watching her?" Colton asked.

Mr. Everett raised his chin, but there was a quiver there. "You were seeing things."

"But I wasn't," Sarah continued. "Were you memorizing her schedule?"

"No!" His voice nearly came out as a yell. Then his shoulders fell, and he squeezed the skin between his eyes. "I loved her."

Silence feel around them. Had Sarah just heard that correctly?

"You what?" Sarah asked.

"I loved her." Mr. Everett shook his head, grief seeming to overtake him. "I wanted to tell her how I felt, but I was always too chicken to do so."

"And that's why you were watching her?" Sarah repeated, disbelief stretching through her voice. Could he actually be telling the truth?

"Yes. Why would I kill her? I have everything I could want. I made millions in the stock market. I have a big house, but no one to share it with. I'm retired. I just wanted a companion." Tears rimmed his eyes. "I would never, ever hurt Loretta. Never. In fact, I'll miss our talks. Loretta was spirited and passionate. I haven't met many women like her."

Reality settled on Sarah. This man was telling the truth. Mr. Everett wouldn't hurt Loretta, and he hadn't seen anything else at the house that evening.

Disappointment bit at her.

"I'm sorry to have upset you," Sarah said, taking a step back. "And I'm sorry for your loss."

Mr. Everett looked away and said nothing.

"Did your son know Loretta?" Colton asked.

Mr. Everett's eyebrows shot up. "My son? What does he have to do with this?"

"I'm just asking a question."

"No, he's never even met her. I just moved here three years ago. He was already in California, and he hasn't been back to visit since then."

"I'm…sorry," Sarah said, her voice soft. "Are you going to call the police on us?"

Mr. Everett remained silent a moment, a frown tugging at the sides of his mouth. "I don't have much choice. It's my duty as a citizen. Why don't you let the justice system prove your innocence?"

"I might have to eventually. But, until then, I need to

find answers. Loretta asked for my help. She asked me to take care of Buzz. And I don't want to let her down."

"I suppose that's admirable."

Colton took Sarah's elbow, seeming ready to usher her away from this area.

But Sarah looked back at Mr. Everett one more time. "At least give us a head start. Because I didn't kill Loretta. I cared about her also. I'm just trying to figure out who's responsible."

After a moment of thought, Mr. Everett nodded. "You've got five minutes until I call the police and tell them what happened when they arrive. And find her killer for me. Please. Because Loretta deserves justice."

Just as he said the words, sirens sounded in the distance.

Colton grabbed Sarah's hand. "Come on. We've gotta get out of here. Now."

Sarah swallowed back her panic.

She wasn't sure which she feared more: the police or the bad guy catching her.

Either way, she'd be a goner.

And that thought only made her move faster.

NINETEEN

Colton knew he, Sarah and Buzz were on borrowed time. If he didn't move now, it might be too late.

"There's a lane behind my house that leads to the highway," Mr. Everett said, pointing in the distance. "Take that. It will give you a little bit of a head start, at least."

Colton hoped the man was telling the truth and not setting them up. "Thank you," he muttered, giving him a final nod.

Then Colton grabbed Sarah's hand and they darted to his truck, climbed inside and quickly tugged on their seat belts.

He was going to have to ditch this vehicle soon, he realized. It was too easily recognizable by now. But Colton would have to think about that later— he didn't want to add car theft to his list of offenses.

Colton knew, deep down inside, that he might not even have a career in law enforcement when all this was done. As far as police were concerned, he was harboring a fugitive. He could be charged as an accessory to a crime.

Casting those thoughts aside, he pressed the accelerator and took off toward the back of the property. He prayed that he didn't regret this. There was no time to think—only to react. Colton just had to move if he wanted all of them to get out of this in one piece.

"You okay?" He glanced at Sarah and saw her holding on to the armrest, her eyes wide and her skin pale.

"I... I guess." She didn't sound convinced.

They'd have to talk more about it later.

Colton reached the end of the lane and held his breath. Finally, he spotted the road that Mr. Everett had told him about. Thank goodness.

It was probably used by hunters who wanted to access the woods at the back of the property during the season.

Colton turned onto it. He hoped to loop around and avoid the police. Most of all, he prayed this wasn't a trap—a dead-end road where they wouldn't be able to get away.

"How'd they find us?" Sarah asked, sounding breathless as she stared straight ahead, looking dazed.

Buzz lay down on the seat behind them and let out a little whine. The canine obviously didn't like this. Neither did Colton.

"I don't know," Colton said. "I'm sure there's an all-points bulletin for my truck. Did Loretta's house have some kind of alarm system maybe?"

"Yes, but it was disabled when we went inside. That shouldn't have triggered anything."

"I don't know. It doesn't matter right now. All that matters is that we get away."

A few minutes of silence passed as the landscape blurred past—lots of trees covered in snow, and occasional glimpses of a river in the distance. Any other day, this drive would be beautiful—the landscape was untouched.

But not right now.

"Colton, I know I've said this before, but I'm really sorry I pulled you into this." Sarah crossed her arms over her chest, her voice wispy with emotion.

Colton hated to see her looking so guilty, so burdened. She blamed herself for too much—for her dad leaving, for her mom being put in jail, for her sister being sent to a different foster home. She just seemed so alone.

"It's okay, Sarah," he told her. "I'm a grown man. I don't do anything I don't want to do."

As he saw three police cars drive past, Colton pulled onto the highway, going in the opposite direction.

He released a breath.

They were clear—for the moment. But Colton knew it wouldn't last long.

"Where are you going now?" Sarah asked, glancing around as if trying to gather her wits. This area had a few little shops and restaurants dotting the streets. Colton didn't know the streets well, but he needed to figure it out quickly.

"We don't have any choice but to hide until this situation clears. We've got to figure out another plan, and I need a new vehicle to drive. We're not safe in this one anymore."

Sarah's jaw clenched as she stared out the window. She was scared.

And she needed to be. When a person felt fear, their survival instincts kicked in. Those instincts could keep people alive as they chose either fight or flight.

Sarah had chosen fight.

Much like Buzz. The dog had great intuition. Without Buzz, they might not be alive right now. He'd alerted them to the man in the park, essentially saving Sarah's life. He'd tried to protect Loretta. He'd won the trust of Mr. Everett.

Buzz was more than a pet or even just an emotional support dog. He was a protector—and that was just the kind of dog Colton could admire.

"What do you think about that letter Loretta left you?" Colton asked, interested in getting her feedback now that the letter had time to sink in.

Loretta's words had touched Colton. The woman had seen the real Sarah—the one who was kind and artistic. Sarah wasn't the killer people were making her out to be. Thank goodness Loretta had seen all the potential in her.

Sarah shook her head. "I really don't know. I had no idea she felt that way about me. Honestly, she was always fussing. I didn't think she liked me at all."

"Your love for Buzz made an impression on her."

Sarah shook her head. "It makes me so sad to realize how, even with all of her success, she felt so lonely in her last days."

"She had you."

"She did, but I was hired help. I... I guess I don't know how I feel yet."

Colton took a quick right onto another road as he saw another police car ahead. He held his breath, waiting to see flashing police lights. Waiting for a chase.

There was none.

The cop car turned the opposite direction.

Colton wasn't sure they were going to get out of this without being caught. But he was going to try to do everything in his power to make it happen.

Sarah closed her eyes and said prayer after prayer.

She didn't want to be caught. Didn't want to go to prison.

But she really didn't want to ruin Colton's life either. Maybe she cared about him more than she'd ever realized. Because the thought of turning his life upside down broke her heart in two.

Colton didn't deserve this. He hadn't done anything. No, she'd pulled him into this crazy situation, and now Sarah needed to figure out a way to get him out.

Sarah stared out the window at the darkening landscape. They were driving deeper into the heart of the mountains, deeper into the countryside and away from Spokane. Was this how she'd spend the rest of her life? She'd either be arrested and potentially go to jail for a crime she didn't commit—or she would have to go into hiding.

Neither option was appealing.

As Colton took another sharp turn, she grabbed the bar above the door and held on. She trusted Colton as a driver. He was always calm, always in control. He always made her feel safe.

But this whole situation had her on edge.

Crime wasn't her world. Art was. She liked to create beautiful things.

But somehow everything had been turned upside down.

Sarah said more prayers and glanced behind her.

She didn't see any police cars headed their way.

Maybe they'd lost them.

For a while.

Colton also glanced into the rearview mirror. As he did, his shoulders seemed to relax and lower—just slightly. If circumstances were different, she might reach over and try to ease some of the tautness from his back.

But those times were past. Not even his sweet kiss on the forehead would change that.

Sarah looked in the backseat at Buzz. The dog was sleeping—finally. He seemed to be working security detail constantly, never letting down his guard. It would be good that everyone was breathing easier, if only for a minute.

"Are we going back to your friend's cabin?" Sarah asked.

"That's the plan. For now. It's the only safe place I can think of. At least we can regroup there."

The idea of being safe had never felt so tempting. All she wanted was to relax. To pretend like nothing was happening.

What she wouldn't do to turn back time. And just how far would she go if she could?

Maybe she would go back two years. Maybe she should have never broken up with Colton. If Sarah hadn't broken up with Colton, she wouldn't be in this mess right now. No, she'd probably have a safe home to return to. Someone to watch her back. The life she'd always wanted. But she'd sabotaged herself.

That was it, wasn't it? She'd been so afraid of getting hurt that she'd jumped the gun and tried to end their relationship before her worst-case scenarios were played out.

But she couldn't forget the issues they'd faced. It hadn't been all sunshine and roses, no matter how much Sarah might want to paint the past like that.

It was too easy to forget how withdrawn Colton had become during his crisis. Too easy to forget their problems. The warning flags that had been raised in her mind.

"What are you thinking about?" Colton asked, his voice soft and prodding.

Sarah swallowed hard. Should she tell him?

No, she decided. Her thoughts were too vulnerable. Colton would laugh at her. He'd obviously moved on. Bought a house. Started a new job. Dealt with the emotional blow that had happened when he was a Seattle detective.

"Just…everything," she finally said, glancing down at her hands in her lap.

"That's a lot."

She managed a wry smile. "Yes, it is. I miss the days of worrying about whether or not I would sell a painting."

"Life has a tendency to put things in perspective sometimes."

"Aren't you worried about your career, Colton?"

He remained quiet a moment before offering a half shrug. "Maybe a little."

She appreciated his honesty.

"But we're going to prove you didn't do this, Sarah," he continued. "Then we'll both be cleared."

Just as he said the words, his phone rang.

He glanced at the screen and frowned.

"Who is it?" Sarah asked, already expecting the worst.

"It's one of my contacts with Spokane Police Department."

She sucked in a deep breath at his words. That couldn't be a good sign. No way. "Are you going to answer?"

He frowned again and raked a hand through his hair before nodding. "Yeah, I better. I can only avoid the truth for so long."

TWENTY

"Hey, Manning," Colton said. "What's going on?"

Manning's voice came through the truck's Bluetooth. Any other time, Colton might have pulled over to talk, but he couldn't afford to lose momentum. They needed to keep moving right now.

"Colton, I just got an all-points bulletin for a truck. The license plate indicates the vehicle is registered to you."

He sucked in a breath. That was the last thing he wanted to hear, yet he wasn't surprised. It had only been a matter of time. He didn't want to own up to anything. Not yet. He wanted more answers first.

"I'm sorry to hear that," Colton said, trying to choose his words carefully.

"Should I be concerned?" Manning continued.

Colton's jaw tightened as he stared at the road, apprehension building in his chest. "Manning, you guys are looking at the wrong person. Sarah Peterson didn't have anything to do with Loretta Blanchard's death."

"Then why is she running? It's usually the first sign of guilt."

"Maybe because she doesn't want to take the fall for a crime she didn't commit. Loretta warned her not to trust the cops."

"Why would she say that?"

"Maybe because a dirty cop was involved in her death."

Manning paused. "And just so we're straight, you're helping her?"

Colton hesitated again. "I'm looking for answers."

"Colton, I've got to tell you that the evidence is pretty clear that she's behind this. Her prints were on the murder weapon. She was seen leaving the scene. She took money with her."

"That doesn't mean she's guilty. She saw a man in Loretta's room. She was set up."

"Why don't you bring her in and let her tell us her side of the story?"

Colton glanced at Sarah. She stared at him, looking like she was barely breathing.

"That's her choice," he finally said.

"You must have feelings for this woman."

Feelings? Did Colton still have feelings for Sarah? "My feelings don't matter right now."

"Just a little advice—don't throw your career away for a woman. You willing to go to jail for this woman?"

Colton squeezed the steering wheel tighter, desperately wishing Sarah wasn't here to overhear this conversation. "If that's what has to happen."

"I wish you hadn't said that."

"You'll see, Manning. She's innocent."

Manning's voice dipped, and he sounded almost apologetic. "Until then, as far as I'm concerned, you're both guilty. And my guys are going to find you."

"How about, instead, you try to find out who the cop is who's involved?"

Before Manning could respond, Colton ended the call and felt the burden of the whole situation press on him.

Beside him, Sarah stared out the window, not saying a word—which was worse than her giving him an earful.

Tension stretched between the two of them—tension that he could feel with every pulse of his heart.

Colton didn't want to admit it, but he knew the truth. He'd never stopped caring about Sarah. And he probably never would. .

Thankfully, the road leading to the cabin came into view. He turned down the gravel lane and headed up the mountain into an even darker darkness.

He paused at the top, just within eyesight of the cabin. From here, the house looked clear.

But Colton would need to check it out before he exposed Sarah and Buzz to whatever might be waiting out of sight.

No one should have found this location. But he was better safe than sorry. Loretta's killer seemed to find them at every turn—first through the phone, then the dog's collar. Who knew what other tricks he had up his sleeve, so to speak?

He put the truck in Park and turned to Sarah. "Wait here."

Then he drew his gun and hopped out. He had to make sure everything was clear.

And then he needed to come up with a plan of action. Because what they were doing right now didn't seem to be working.

Sarah reached back to rub Buzz's head as she waited for Colton to return.

Colton thought someone might be hiding out inside, just waiting to grab them or arrest them or kill them for that matter. The thought wasn't comforting.

Nor was that phone call. It was just like Sarah had suspected. Colton was in serious trouble for helping her. She should have never pulled him into this. But now it was too late. He was in too deep.

"What are we going to do, Buzz?" she murmured.

The dog nuzzled her hand in response, seeming to sense her distress.

A moment later, Colton stepped onto the porch and motioned that it was safe for them to come inside.

Sarah climbed from his truck, waiting as Buzz hopped out beside her. Though Colton had indicated it was safe, that didn't stop her from moving quickly. Her body felt programmed to expect danger. As soon as she was inside, a wave of relief filled her.

For a moment—and just a moment—she felt safe. And she'd never realized just how much she valued that feeling until now.

"We should have grabbed something to eat while we were out," Colton said. "It looks like it will be canned soup again."

"I'm grateful just to have food," she said. And she meant it. If she was doing this on her own…she'd probably be dead right now. Or starving. Or cold.

So many things.

Colton smiled, a nostalgic look drifting through his gaze. "You always were content with the simple things."

"I guess when you've lived with absolutely nothing, you learn to be." The words caught in her throat.

She didn't like to talk about her past. She didn't want people to feel sorry for her. But her past contained so many answers about why she was the way she was today. All of those heartaches had shaped her. Then God's grace had smoothed some of the rough edges. That grace was still smoothing rough edges.

Colton's smile faded. "Yeah, I guess so. So what will it be? Chicken noodle or vegetable beef?"

"Vegetable beef sounds great."

"I'll cook then."

Sarah went over to the fireplace and added logs. It had been a long time since she'd actually started a fire. After finding the lighter, she managed to successfully start the flames. Once they were sufficiently fanned and the logs were burning, she stepped back, satisfied with her work.

She lowered herself near the fire and pulled a blanket over her legs to ward away the cold. The scent of the soup filled the cabin and created a lovely atmosphere, despite their circumstances.

There had always been something about log cabins that she loved, that made her feel warm and cozy inside. In fact, living in a place like this—or even in a cabin like Colton's—would be so perfect.

As long as she had her art supplies, of course.

Why had she ever thought anything otherwise? She'd had everything she wanted and needed right in front of her. She'd been such a fool. And now it was too late to ever make things right, wasn't it?

"You were brave today, Sarah," Colton said across the room.

She felt the heat rise on her cheeks. "I don't know about brave. Maybe just determined."

"No, you were brave. A lot of people would be crushed by now, but not you."

"Thank you," she finally said, unsure of what else to say.

Colton paused from stirring the soup. "You look beautiful, Sarah."

Sarah blinked. Had she heard him correctly? Certainly not, because Colton had told her when they broke up that if she left, they were done for good. And Colton was always a man of his word.

So why in the world had he said those words just now?

Either way, it would be better if Sarah forgot them, along with all the feelings that had begun stirring inside her chest.

Besides, she needed to focus on clearing her name and finding Loretta's killer. Nothing could distract her from that.

Not even Colton.

Especially not Colton.

Colton clamped his mouth shut as he continued to stir the soup. Why had he said that?

He wasn't even sure where the words came from. They'd just left his lips before he had a chance to stop them—and that was something that never happened. Colton was always one to choose his words carefully.

But something changed in him when he was around Sarah.

And looking at her just now with the plaid blanket around her, with Buzz at her feet, with the fireplace bathing her skin in hues of orange and yellow…it made his dreams come alive again.

For better or worse.

A flustered look crossed Sarah's face, and she looked like she tried to smile but failed. Instead, she stood and went to the fireplace to stoke the logs again—probably desperate to avoid his gaze.

He couldn't blame her.

A few minutes later, they were seated in front of the fire with soup in hand. Colton had made some rice and gravy for Buzz also, and he happily ate from a bowl in the kitchen.

For a moment—and just a moment—things felt normal. He and Sarah sitting here and eating together felt normal, like old times.

His heart raced when he realized it was anything but.

"Do you miss police work?" Sarah asked.

Colton nodded slowly. "Yeah, I actually do. Sometimes. But the break has been good for me."

Sarah stole a glance at him, her gaze softening. "I know that last investigation was really hard on you."

He ate another bite of his soup and took his time swallowing, chewing on his response for a moment. "Yeah, it was. But I've been through counseling, and I'm doing better."

"I'm glad."

Colton would have been doing even better if Sarah had stuck with him. She'd given up on their relationship so easily. Given up on him.

They could have had such a great life together. Sarah had brought something out in him that made him feel alive. That made Colton want to explore the unknown. To relax instead of working all the time. To seek out the beauty in life. And Colton liked to think that he'd offered Sarah security and protection and love.

But maybe that hadn't been enough.

She glanced at her hands. "You know, after seeing Loretta…die…and then seeing Frank…it makes me understand what you went through a little more. It's not easy seeing someone lose his or her life…and I can't imagine being in the position you were in."

Colton cleared this throat, touched by her words. "It's not easy. In fact, it can be crippling."

"I'm sorry I wasn't there for you."

His heart pounded in his ears at her soft words. Just that one sentence seemed to unleash something in him. But he still held back, still waited.

"What's next for you, Sarah?" he asked. "When all of this is over?"

"Assuming this ends well?"

"Assuming life goes back to some semblance of normal."

Colton studied Sarah as he waited for her answer. She looked adorable as she sat there. She'd pulled her hair back into a ponytail, making her seem even more youthful than her twenty-seven years.

This was the Sarah he missed.

She paused with her spoon halfway to her mouth. "It's hard to say. I'll no longer have a job. I probably won't be able to find one in Spokane now that my name has been dragged through the mud."

"So you'll move?" He had to keep talking to her like this would end well. He had to keep hope alive. But he knew deep down inside that this whole situation might not have the closure they both longed for.

Sarah shrugged. "Maybe. I haven't even thought about it. There have been several times I've thought about going back to waitressing. It's not a lot of money, but at least it's a paycheck."

The thought of Sarah throwing her dreams away twisted his insides. "I don't want to sound like a broken record, but you have a lot of talent, Sarah. You should pursue it."

She shrugged. "Why does it really matter anymore? All my work is gone. I've been trying so hard, and nothing has come from it except heartache. Maybe I should take that as a sign. In fact, maybe the writing has been on the wall for a long time."

"Sarah…"

"It's true. Besides, you and I both know that all of this is going to change everything. Who knows if we'll even get out of this situation alive…"

"I'm going to do everything I can to protect you, Sarah."

A sad smile tugged at her lips. "Thank you."

"Further, you'll have some of Loretta's money at the end of this. That's probably several million dollars."

"I don't want her money." Sarah shook her head, moisture

flooding her eyes as she remembered all the events leading up to that realization.

"Really?" Not many people would turn down that amount of money.

"Really. I don't… I don't know. I don't deserve it."

"Why would you say that?"

She swiped a stray hair behind her ear. "I didn't know Loretta that well, for starters. And money usually comes with strings attached, you know?"

Colton wondered if Sarah was thinking about the job she'd moved to Spokane for. The one where her boss had expected more than she'd promised. The thought of it still made anger burn in him. "What if there aren't any strings attached?"

She put her mug down, pulled her knees to her chest and shrugged. "I don't really know. I really just wish Loretta was back. I'd rather have people in my life than money."

"I know you would, Sarah."

"I've missed you, Colton." Suddenly Sarah's cheeks flushed and she looked away, a hand going to her forehead like she tried to cover her embarrassment. "I'm sorry. I don't know where that came from."

"I've missed you too, Sarah." His heart panged with longing that he'd tried to bury for so long.

Without thinking—or overthinking—he reached over and put his arm around Sarah, pulling her toward him until her head hit his chest. He hated thinking about her being all alone. He couldn't stop thinking about Loretta's words in that letter—about how they'd shared being all alone in the world. No one should have to say that.

To his surprise, Sarah nestled into him, nearly melting in his embrace.

It felt so good to have her close. To breathe in her honeysuckle scent. To feel her silky hair beneath his chin.

"Colton?"

His breath caught. "Yes?"

Sarah raised her head. "I just thought you should know that letting you go was one of the biggest mistakes I've ever made."

Her words washed over him, causing his heart to thump out of control. Her affirmation was all he needed to confirm that they both still had feelings for each other…feelings that might be worth exploring again.

Colton reached up, his hand brushing her jaw. Her neck. Her cheek

Sarah was so beautiful. And so perfect for him.

His lips met hers, and all the feelings they'd once shared for each other seemed to explode in one sweet moment.

This was Sarah. His Sarah. The only person he'd ever wanted to be with.

Except she wasn't his.

The thought nearly made Colton's muscles freeze.

He couldn't go through another heartache like the one he'd experienced when they broke up. He couldn't.

Colton pulled away and looked down at the floor. "I'm sorry. I shouldn't have done that."

His words seemed to startle Sarah, and she drew back, her eyes fluttering again with embarrassment. "You're right. Of course not. I don't know what we were thinking."

As the words left her mouth, she stood and grabbed their mugs. "I should clean up."

And then Sarah was gone.

Colton bit down. He'd messed that up. Or had he? He knew he needed to keep his distance, as hard as it might be. When he saw Sarah, there was nothing more that he wanted to do than step back in time. He wanted to pretend that nothing had changed. That they were still together.

But that wasn't the case. She'd broken his heart, and he'd be wise to remember that.

Then why was Colton's heart telling him otherwise?

His jaw tightened.

None of this was supposed to happen. When Sarah walked away, he'd figured she was gone for good. Now they'd been thrown together in these fantastical circumstances.

Colton just needed to concentrate on the goal right now—keeping Sarah alive. That was all that was important. And the task was becoming harder with every day that passed. It had become obvious that the person behind Loretta's murder would stop at nothing to reach Sarah.

And as the noose tightened, Colton needed every bit of his focus to be on this investigation. Their lives depended on it.

TWENTY-ONE

Sarah put the mugs in the sink and began to furiously clean them.

What had she been thinking? Why had she ever even let herself dream that they might have a second chance?

She knew Colton better than that. Knew that once he said they were done, they were done. Yet foolishly she'd allowed herself to think about another future with him. His momentary look of desire had quickly been replaced with a look of hurt.

The thing was that she couldn't even blame him for not giving her a second chance. She was the one who'd messed up things between them, and she'd be a fool to ever think otherwise.

"You know, I'm going to take a shower since we still have water," she said once the dishes were done.

"Okay then. I'll keep watch out here and maybe let Buzz out."

"That sounds perfect." Really, she would take any excuse she could find to get away from the man.

As she stepped toward the bathroom door, Colton called her name.

She paused and glanced at him.

He opened his mouth, as if there were things he wanted to say. Then he shut it again.

"It's okay, Colton," Sarah said. "You don't have to say anything. Really."

Before he could try to force any more conversation, Sarah stepped into the bathroom. As soon as the door closed, she leaned against it, feeling the effects of humiliation and regret.

If she even managed to get out of this situation without jail time, her future seemed so bleak.

Colton nearly kicked himself for messing that up.

But maybe it had been the right thing. Usually these issues were so much clearer to him.

Why did everything feel like it was upside down now that Sarah had come back into his life?

He called Buzz. "Let's go outside, boy."

Colton would let the dog stretch while also keeping an eye on the place. Maybe cooling off was the best thing he could do right now.

After slipping his boots back on and tugging on a coat, he stepped into the frigid winter wonderland outside his door. The blackness around him—even though he should be used to it—still felt unnerving after everything that had happened.

He hadn't really had the chance to explore this property, though he did know that his friend owned about thirty acres. The two went way back. In fact, Jack had dated Colton's sister at one time, and he and Jack had remained friends. However, the connection was so distant that Colton didn't think the police would find him here.

But Colton didn't know how long they'd be safe at this location. He needed to keep thinking of other ideas.

Because he was fully invested in this now. Despite what

had just happened between him and Sarah, Colton wouldn't turn his back on her.

He saw a barn in the distance and decided to check out that area, just in case they ever needed it.

Buzz trotted along beside him as he tromped through the snow.

With one last glance back at the house, Colton pulled the barn door open and stepped inside.

A truck was parked there.

Colton went to it and tugged the driver's side door. To his surprise, it opened.

His friend must store this here for off-roading. It didn't surprise Colton.

He climbed into the driver's seat. After reaching under the front seat, Colton found the keys.

Country living at its finest. People out here didn't give a second thought to leaving their keys hidden.

He placed them back under the seat and stepped back out into the barn.

"We should probably get back inside now, huh, boy?" he asked the dog.

Buzz wagged his tail in response.

Colton stepped outside, closing the barn door beside him. He glanced around as he walked back toward the cabin, but he saw nothing unusual. Heard nothing unusual.

He had a hard time thinking that someone could track them down here. They just needed a safe place to stay until they could collect their thoughts.

A safe place…

That was all Sarah said she wanted.

And if she didn't feel safe, she fled, didn't she?

He could hardly blame her considering how she'd grown up.

He stepped inside and heard that the water was off in the bathroom. While he had a free moment, he did a quick online search for Yvonne, Loretta's biggest competitor, and then sent a few emails, including one to Detective Simmons, letting him know what was going on.

A moment later, the door opened, followed by a cloud of steam. Sarah stepped out with her wet hair falling around her face and her skin looking clean and refreshed.

She offered a shy smile.

Colton's heart thudded out of control.

If he was smart, he would grab on to her and never let her go. He would fight for another chance at a relationship with everything inside him.

Was it his pride that stood in the way?

Before he could examine the question any further, Buzz's hair stood on end, and he growled at the front of the cabin.

Colton and Sarah exchanged a look.

Buzz knew something they didn't.

Buzz knew someone else was here.

TWENTY-TWO

Sarah watched as Colton's eyes widened.

Something was wrong.

He grabbed some water and doused out the fire, leaving them in almost complete blackness.

"Put your shoes and jacket on," he whispered.

She did as he instructed, too scared to argue.

"Stay down," Colton said.

Sarah dropped down behind the couch, her skin crawling with fear.

What was going on? What had Buzz heard?

The dog was smart enough to only alert if there was real danger.

There must be someone outside.

And if that man had the chance, he'd kill them. This could be the opportunity when nothing stopped him.

Colton glanced out the window. "He's here."

"What's he doing?"

"I don't know," Colton said. "I don't see him right now. I only see that he parked his sedan behind the truck."

"He blocked us in," Sarah muttered.

"That's what it looks like."

Sarah sniffed, a new scent filling the air. She gasped. "Colton, is that—"

"Gasoline," he finished. "He's going to set this place on fire."

Colton burst from his position near the window and darted toward her. He took her hand and pulled her toward the back door. She barely had time to grab her purse and Buzz's bag before he threw the back door open.

As he did, a ball of flames exploded around them. They leaped over the fire just as it started around them, before landing in the snow.

They didn't have time to stop. Colton pulled Sarah to her feet and called for Buzz to follow.

He grabbed a branch from an evergreen tree near the deck and broke it off. Using the needles there, he covered the tracks behind them as they ran into the barn and climbed into a truck there.

"What's this doing here?" Sarah asked, stopping for a minute to stare in awe.

"I don't know, but I found it earlier."

"What's our plan?" she continued.

"That man will probably check the house."

"Is he trying to kill us?"

"Or smoke us out. Either way, we to need to get out of here soon."

"I can't believe this is happening." A tremble claimed her voice.

"Hold tight," Colton said. "Because once we leave, we're getting out of here and not looking back. I'm not going to give this guy time to find us."

She pulled on her seat belt. "Whatever you say."

But she had her doubts they were going to be able to pull this off. The stakes were too high. This guy was too relentless.

She lifted a prayer that Colton's plan would work. If it didn't, she had no idea what else to do.

* * *

Colton climbed from the truck and peered out a crack in the barn door.

In the distance, he saw his friend's cabin going up in flames.

He was going to have a lot of explaining to do. Colton had never intended on this happening. But that man had found them—again.

What were they missing?

It didn't matter right now. All that mattered was getting out of here.

Movement caught his eye.

It was the man.

He was checking out his work by walking around the house.

Colton wasn't sure if his footprint cover-up had worked. Maybe he'd bought them a little time, at least.

Just as the thought entered his mind, the man paused.

He saw the tracks, Colton realized.

And the man was following them to the barn.

Colton waited until the man was halfway there. Too soon, and he'd allow the man too much time. Too late, and they'd be sitting ducks.

Now he just had to pray that the truck started.

He rushed back to it and climbed inside.

Lifting a prayer, he put the key in the ignition.

The truck started.

Thank You, Jesus.

Wasting no more time, he put the truck in Drive and pressed the accelerator.

"What are you doing?" Sarah asked, again holding on for dear life.

"Sorry—but brace yourself." The truck burst through the barn doors.

As it did, the man froze just outside the structure before diving out of the way.

Colton didn't slow down. He charged forward, moving as quickly as he could.

Soon, the tires hit the gravel lane leading to the cabin. Then the tires hit the road.

He glanced in his rearview mirror.

Headlights lit the dark.

The man was going to follow them.

But Colton had a head start. He needed to utilize it as much as he could.

Their lives depended on it.

TWENTY-THREE

Sarah closed her eyes and prayed. Prayed hard. Prayed harder than she could remember doing in recent years—which said a lot because she'd had many pressing concerns to lift up over…well, over her entire life.

But these back roads were so slick and dark and curvy.

She didn't see how she, Colton and Buzz were going to survive this.

The cabin fire had made it clear that this man was out to kill, and nothing would stop him from getting what he wanted.

As Colton followed the curve of the road, Buzz fell onto her, momentum shifting his body weight.

Sarah leaned into the dog and got a whiff of the piney scent of his shampoo. The scent immediately brought her comfort. This dog had been such a trouper. Sarah felt the need to protect him whatever the cost. Buzz was special to her—and he'd also been so special to Loretta.

Sarah couldn't let her boss down. Taking care of Buzz was nonnegotiable.

"Watch out," Colton muttered.

He made another sharp turn to the left. As the truck righted itself, its tires left the asphalt and churned on gravel instead. They climbed a steep incline, and the road narrowed in front of them as they snaked up higher and higher.

"Where are we?" Sarah asked, looking around, her heart pounding.

"This is an old logging road."

"What if it's a dead end? What if we're trapped?"

"Let's pray that's not the case." Colton kept moving forward, the tires crunching the rocks beneath them as they sped out of sight and into further isolation.

Sarah looked back, expecting to see headlights.

She saw nothing but darkness.

Had they lost the man? Could she even hope?

She wouldn't breathe easier for a while. No, there was too much at stake.

The road seemed so treacherous, and blackness surrounded them. At any moment, the path in front of them could end at a cliff, undetectable in their vision.

Even if the man didn't directly kill them, there were still so many other dangers.

Please, Lord, help us now! I beg You. We're out of options.

"You have no idea where this road leads?" Sarah muttered, still trying to find hope in this situation as alarms sounded in her head.

"No idea. Probably a field or clearing."

That wasn't what she wanted to hear. "Does it cut through to another road?"

"Also no idea."

Sarah's anxiety continued to rise at the great unknown before them. "Maybe I can check your phone. Maybe a map feature will show us where we are and where we're going."

"There's no service out here."

"Colton…" Her voice came out as a wispy gasp. There

was no need to try to conceal her fear any longer. Her life was flashing before her eyes.

"We're going to be okay."

Colton kept saying that. But did he really believe it? Because nothing in her life had been okay. Nothing. She had nothing and no one. Not even her paintings. Not even the woman who'd let her live in her house.

When this was over, Sarah had nowhere to go and nothing to do to earn money.

She swallowed the despair that wanted to consume her.

Colton muttered something under his breath before swerving to the left.

Ice slid beneath the wheels, and they careened into the darkness.

As Colton tapped the brakes, the truck glided toward the blackness.

Toward what was a cliff at the edge of the road.

She closed her eyes, certain they were going to die.

Colton pressed the brakes, holding his breath as the unthinkable began to play out.

The truck began to slide on the icy ground beneath them.

No! They hadn't come this far for this. No way. He couldn't let it happen.

Dear God, I need Your assistance right now. Desperately. Unequivocally.

Gently, he turned the wheel, trying to veer them away from the edge of the cliff that would mean certain death.

They inched closer and closer, moving as if in slow motion.

No, Lord...please, help us!

The truck was out of his control and at the mercy of the ice...and God.

Sarah reached over and grabbed his hand, squeezing it as if her life was depending on it.

They both seemed to hold their breath as they watched and waited.

Only a few inches shy of the drop-off, the truck stopped.

Stopped.

It didn't fall.

The vehicle stood still, completely upright and safe.

Colton released the air from his lungs and felt his shoulders sag with relief. They were okay. They were really okay.

That had been close.

Too close.

He glanced over at Sarah and Buzz, checking to see how they were doing. Sarah looked pale but otherwise okay.

Buzz let out a little bark, as if telling Colton he wasn't happy with him right now.

But they were safe, and that was all that mattered.

Colton raked a hand through his hair.

"I thought we were going to die," Sarah finally muttered, her head dropping against the seat behind her.

"But we didn't."

She turned toward him, her eyes full of questions. "What now?"

Survival instincts pounded with each pulse of his heart, and adrenaline rushed through him. "We're going to keep heading down this road—at a slower pace. We're going to see where it leads, and then we'll probably just have to park somewhere for the night and conceal the truck."

"And then?"

He desperately wanted to tell Sarah they were going to get through this unscathed. But he couldn't do that because the closer danger pressed, the more he realized how precarious this situation was.

"And then we figure out what we can do in the morning."

"What if that man finds us here?"

Colton had thought about that. The man was smart. He was no doubt looking for them now. The good news was that there were a lot of logging roads like this in the area.

"I do know that in this area, there are no cell phone signals. It's pretty remote. There's a good chance that if he's tracking us using technology, which is what I suspect he's doing, he won't be able to get a read on our location."

"Most likely?"

He shrugged. "I wish I could offer more, but I don't want to lie to you."

"I appreciate that." Sarah crossed her arms and looked out the window. "I guess we should get going then."

Good. Sarah was staying strong and trying not to panic. Those two traits would go a long way.

TWENTY-FOUR

It took several minutes for Sarah's heart to stop pounding out of control. But Colton had slowed down, and the road right now wasn't nestled up to the edge of a cliff. She could breathe a little easier.

Silence fell in the truck. Buzz lay between them, his head in Sarah's lap. Since the dog was relaxing, it seemed a good sign that Sarah should be able to relax also. No cars followed them. There didn't appear to be any more patches of ice. Just a quiet nighttime drive through the countryside.

In different circumstances, this would seem like an adventure. A chance to see the crystal clear sky above and the stars nestled there. To listen to the sounds of the forest at night. The payoffs would include a campfire and moments of heart-to-heart talks and dreaming about the future.

Those things had changed when she and Colton had split. She hadn't realized how much she missed those times.

Ten minutes later, Colton hit the brakes again and backed into a small clearing between some trees. "Seems as good a place as any to set up camp for the night."

"If you say so."

Without saying anything more, Colton hopped out, found some branches and covered the front of the truck.

He then climbed back in and took Buzz out for a bathroom break.

Sarah listened in silence for a moment.

And that's what it was around here—quiet. There was nothing to hear except for Colton and Buzz walking. A few minutes later, they were back, and Colton turned toward her.

"We should be safe here for a little while," Colton said. His breath already caused a frosty puff to form in front of his face. "We should try to get some rest because who knows what tomorrow holds."

As a brisk wind swept in with the open door, it brought Colton's leathery scent. For a moment, Sarah craved his closeness. His warmth.

Too bad what she craved could never be hers.

"I suppose none of us know what tomorrow holds," she finally said. "Isn't that what the Bible says?"

He nodded slowly, looking weary for the first time since all of this began. "Yes, it is. And then the Bible goes on to tell us that we shouldn't worry."

Sarah crossed her arms, longing for a blanket and a warm drink. She wished for her Bible so she could read it, and maybe even a good devotional book to remind her of what to do when she got off track.

"It feels impossible not to worry in a situation like this one," she said. "I'm trying to cast all my cares upon the Lord, but it's so hard sometimes."

"God knows the path set before us," Colton said. "It's hard to keep that in mind sometimes, though. I've lost sight of it many times."

"Yes, it is hard to remember." Her faith in God had been all that had gotten her through many difficult seasons. But she felt like she was floundering right now, uncertain about everything.

A few seconds ticked by. Tension stretched between them. Unspoken conversations battled to surface. The desire to relive the past warred inside them both.

Sarah longed to feel the warmth Colton offered. To share sweet kisses and promises of tomorrow. But the reality was that she and Colton were better off keeping their walls up.

"Sarah, about earlier—"

She had to stop Colton before it went any further. The last thing she needed was a clumsy explanation or an awkward conversation. "You don't have to explain. You really don't."

That last case—it was the one that had changed everything. That had turned their relationship upside down. That had driven an invisible wedge between them that neither had conquered.

"I know…it's just that after that last case…" Colton started, his voice taking on a new kind of exhaustion.

"Every officer told you they would have done exactly what you did given the situation."

Colton glanced down at his hands, calloused from hard work. "I know. But I killed a man in front of his wife and kids."

She could hear how haunted his voice still sounded. "You tried to stop him. He was about to kill all of you. Besides, I know you tried every method possible to stop him. Shooting him was a last resort. He had his gun drawn on his wife."

His jaw tightened. "She was just so angry afterward, even though she would have died otherwise. She attacked me, yelling. Furious at what I'd done."

"The human mind is complex. You know that."

He nodded. "I do."

"And you just became so distant after that," Sarah continued. "I didn't think you'd ever snap out of it."

"You didn't give me a chance to. You left." His voice sounded hoarse with emotion.

She glanced at her lap. "I probably shouldn't have. But I got scared. I saw what tragedy did to my father. He lost his job, panicked that he couldn't support his family and he became a different person. He left, and the rest of us never recovered. Since I was a kid, I've learned to put up walls to stay safe and not get hurt. When I saw you changing into a different person right in front of me..."

Colton grabbed her hand, his gaze locking with hers. "I wasn't changing. I was just dealing."

"My experiences don't tell me that. My experiences tell me that I should end things before I get hurt. I've already had enough hurt to last a lifetime."

"Sarah..."

Sarah shrugged. "I don't know what else to say. I regret it. There. Are you happy? I miss you. I cried for days, wishing things were different."

"And they could have been." Colton's voice came out soft, full of regret.

She glanced at him. "But I guess it doesn't matter anymore, does it?"

He frowned. "No, I guess it doesn't. What's done is done."

"Or like you always say, it is what it is."

His jaw tightened again, and he turned away. "I guess you and I should both get some sleep."

"We should." She shifted until her back was toward him. "Good night."

"Good night."

Colton had hardly slept the whole night. No, he'd stayed awake, listening and looking for any sign of trouble around them in the carefully hidden truck.

All he saw was darkness.

Colton could only assume that the person following them had some type of electronic device that he used to keep tabs on them. At first it was Sarah's phone. Then it was Buzz's collar.

What was this guy using now?

Colton would need to go through Sarah's purse when she woke up and make sure there were no tracking devices there. This guy continually had the upper hand, and that wasn't okay.

As the nighttime began to fade to gray, his mind wandered to his friend's cabin. Had firefighters come? Had they put the blaze out? It was only a matter of time before the cops realized Colton had been there.

His truck had been parked outside the cabin. The bloody clothes that Sarah had worn on the night of Loretta's murder were inside. No doubt they would look guilty when the cops found that bag—if it hadn't burned up in the flames. It was hard to know exactly how devastating the fire had been.

He glanced at Sarah as she cuddled against the seat with Buzz's head on her lap. She looked like such an angel when she slept, as her blond hair fell in her face and her lips were slightly parted.

He'd give anything to wake up to this sight every morning. If only he could forget about the way she'd hurt him.

He had kissed her…and it had felt wonderful. Too wonderful. He'd been swept back in time to better days. Days that he longed for. Maybe it had even sparked some hope in him.

But should he even let himself go there again?

Logically, Colton knew he shouldn't. But emotionally, he wanted to give them another chance. He wanted to believe they had a future together.

He needed to sort out just how much he was willing to

risk. The last thing he wanted was to have his heart broken again.

Absently, he reached over and rubbed Buzz's back. The dog was sleeping right now, but Colton had no doubt he would be instantly alert if danger came close.

Finally, the sunlight began to peek over the horizon, and the sky turned a misty gray color. Today was supposed to be sunny, and the snowstorms were supposed to have passed—for now.

Colton had to figure out a plan of action here, but he was drawing a blank as to where to go next. There were no clear options. Not in his mind, at least.

Sarah began to stir. Beautiful, sweet Sarah.

It was too bad there was just so much history between them. That the divide was too vast. His heart ached at the thought.

"Morning," he said.

She sat up straight and smoothed out her shirt as she blinked and glanced around. "Morning. I guess we survived."

"We survived."

She yawned and stretched as she tried to wake up. "You didn't see anyone?"

"Not a soul."

Instinctively, it seemed, Sarah reached over and patted Buzz's head. The dog mimicked Sarah by yawning and stretching also. "That's good news, at least."

"I agree."

She turned toward him. "What now?"

"Now I think we should head back to Spokane." He'd been giving it some thought as he'd watched the night pass.

"Really?" Sarah's eyebrows shot up. "What are we going to do there?"

"Last night before the fire, while you were in the shower, I checked online, and it looks like Yvonne is back in town."

She was the next logical person to question. However, the woman could be connected with Loretta's death. If Yvonne was the killer, then she could try to silence Colton and Sarah. If she wasn't the killer, she might call the cops.

It was a risk. Then again, everything about this had been risky. They weren't going to find any answers unless they did things outside their comfort zone.

"You think she'll talk to us?" Sarah asked.

"I think there's only one way we can find out."

Sarah turned toward him, her gaze unwavering. "I'm game then. Let's go."

Colton nodded, glad she was willing. But he also prayed this decision was wise and he wasn't putting them in unnecessary danger. It was one thing if he put himself at risk. But putting Sarah in the line of fire was an entirely different story.

Please, Lord. Keep Sarah safe. Help us find answers. And end this nightmare sooner rather than later.

TWENTY-FIVE

Sarah couldn't stop thinking about the conversation she had with Colton yesterday. So much of what needed to be said had finally been spoken aloud. She was grateful for those conversations, even if they opened up reminders that she'd rather forget.

Reminders about what a good thing they'd had. Reminders about how imperfect they both were. Reminders that there were some obstacles too hard to overcome.

Because she might be trying to convince herself of that, but her heart said otherwise. Her heart told her there was no one else in this world she'd rather be with.

They pulled back onto the road leading to Spokane. She glanced around the mountainy road, getting a better glimpse of it right now in the daylight.

"This area really is so beautiful."

"I love it out here."

"Where you live is nice also."

"I like it. It's quiet, but I'm close enough that I can get places if I need to."

Sarah wondered what it would be like to live up there. Now that she'd seen it with her own eyes, she realized there was a tranquility to the area.

"Sarah, I need you to look through your purse and see if

there's anything there this guy could be tracking us with," Colton said.

"You think that's how he's finding us now?"

"I just know he's resourceful. I want to check all our bases here."

"Of course." She rummaged through everything there but found nothing that looked like a tracking device. She had her wallet, ChapStick, some powder in a compact, a few mints. "There's really nothing."

He let out a grunt. "It just doesn't make sense."

Just as he said the words, a car pulled onto the road right in front of them.

Colton threw on his brakes to stop in time.

Sarah gasped, bracing herself for impact.

The truck halted just in time.

But before they could even catch their breath, Sarah saw that it was a police car.

"Colton…" she muttered.

"Is this a cop who's chasing us down…or the killer?"

A man in uniform stepped out of the driver's seat. With a gun. Pointed at them.

Sarah saw his face, his build and instinctively knew this man was the killer.

He'd finally caught them. And they had nowhere to go.

"Stay behind me," Colton said, eyeing the cop with the gun.

Colton knew he couldn't reach for his own weapon in time. No, the man would shoot all of them before Colton could reach into his waistband and pull it out.

"Get out!" the man yelled.

Colton glanced at Sarah, concerned for her safety.

There was no one out here on this road. Earlier, that had seemed like a great idea. Right now, it seemed like they'd driven right into a trap.

Above them was a tall mountain loaded with snow. On the other side was a cliff.

"I'm scared," Sarah muttered.

"Like I said, just stay behind me," Colton told her.

Slowly, he climbed from the truck, his hands raised. Buzz jumped out behind him and let out a low growl. Colton didn't bother to tell the dog to back off.

Sarah climbed out also, walked around the back of the truck and stood behind Colton, just as he'd directed.

"What do you want?" Colton asked.

The man chuckled. "You still don't know? Really?"

"We have no idea."

"Oh, isn't this smart. You guys were harder to get to than I thought. Kudos for that."

Colton studied the man. He carried himself like a law enforcement officer.

Was this man a cop? It would explain how he'd tracked them so easily. It would also explain why Loretta had said not to trust cops.

But what was this man's connection with Loretta? He had no idea what the man could be after.

Maybe it was the money Sarah was going to inherit from Loretta? It was the only thing that made sense.

"You should have never gone to work for Loretta," the man said, looking at Sarah.

"Why not?" Sarah asked. "What was so bad about working for her?"

"You got yourself in this mess, didn't you?"

"I didn't do anything. I was just taking care of Buzz."

The man chuckled again. "Well, I'm sorry you have to be a part of this, if it's any consolation."

"It's not," Sarah responded. "What are you going to do with us?"

"I have no reason to keep you alive. This isn't the way I wanted to do it, though."

"You should just let us go. Tell us what you want, and we'll be out of your life," Sarah continued.

"It's not that easy."

"Sure it is," Colton said. "We don't want to be a part of this any more than you want us to be a part of it."

"I just need the formula."

Colton and Sarah both froze and glanced at each other.

"What formula?" Colton asked, trying to buy time.

"For the new drug Loretta was developing."

"I don't have the formula," Sarah muttered.

The man scowled. "Yes, you do. We overheard Loretta talking. That's what she said."

"Who was she talking with?" Sarah asked, looking as confused as Colton felt.

"It doesn't matter. What matters is that you have something I want." Patience—if there had been any—disappeared from the man's voice.

"If I do, I don't know where it is." Sarah's voice trembled.

"Come on. Don't make me do this the hard way."

"Why are you trying to kill me?" Sarah asked. "How will you find this information out if I'm dead?"

It was a great question. Colton tried to put the pieces together.

"At least you'd be out of my way. But I haven't been able to find this information anywhere, so it must be on you somewhere."

"Where?" Sarah raised her hands. "I have nothing."

"It's somewhere. Tell me where."

"I don't know," Sarah said.

"Tell me!" The man raised his gun in the air, anger flashing in his gaze.

As the man pulled the trigger, Colton dove over Sarah, protecting her from the shot.

But as soon as they hit the ground, a rumble sounded above them.

Colton looked up just in time to see the start of an avalanche.

TWENTY-SIX

Colton grabbed Sarah's hand and pulled her toward the truck. Buzz remained at their heels.

The terrible rumbling that Sarah heard got her blood racing.

She wasn't sure they were going to make it.

They dove into the truck and Colton threw it into Reverse. Carefully—but quickly—he backed the truck down the curvy mountain road.

Sarah wanted to close her eyes. She didn't want to see—what was in front of her or behind.

Yet she couldn't look away.

The road in front of them already had chunks of snow falling on it—chunks big enough to squash someone.

Her eyes searched for the cop who'd been ready to kill them.

His police car was still on the side of the road. He had just climbed inside.

But the snow had already covered half of it.

She said a prayer.

That man might be evil, but she didn't want to see anyone die.

Swiveling her head again, Sarah glanced behind her and sucked in a deep breath.

Another snow clump, the size of a boulder, hit the side of the cop car. Colton threw the truck into Drive and did a three-point turn. Then he quickly dodged around the snow. Another mass hit the top of the vehicle.

This time Sarah did close her eyes.

This could be the end. She had no doubt about that.

Please, Lord. Help us. I know I keep asking that but I'm at the end of my rope.

More boulder-like pieces of snow and ice hit the road. The truck swerved and slid on the ice, nearly skating across the street.

Sarah grabbed the front of the dashboard, trying to steady herself. Her heart flipped and leaped inside her.

They'd left one danger behind, only to face this.

She drew in some deep breaths, trying to calm down.

A few seconds later, the truck was no longer sliding or swerving.

She dared to open her eyes and glance at Colton. His hands were white-knuckled on the steering wheel. Determination tightened his jaw.

But the road in front of them was clear.

She looked back once more and saw the cloud of snow and ice on the road.

The avalanche had destroyed the windy mountain lane.

But she, Colton and Buzz were okay.

She let out a breath, her thoughts swirling. They were really okay.

"You did it," she told Colton. "You got away."

"Only by the grace of God." Colton glanced behind him. "I'm not sure that guy did."

"No, I can't imagine that's the case." Sarah turned back to him, her voice catching. "Colton, a cop is involved with this. That's why Loretta warned me. This appears to be tied in with Loretta's drug company after all." Sarah shook her head in disbelief.

"Are you wearing any jewelry Loretta gave you? Do you have a credit card? Anything?"

"No, just that money that was in the backpack I took with me when I left Loretta's house with Buzz."

"Somehow, someway, this guy thought you had the formula. That's why he's been chasing us. The man also used the word *we*. That means he's working with someone."

Sarah stared out the window. "I just have no idea who that would be."

Colton handed her his phone. "Why don't you see if there's any new information in the news today? It might be our best source at this point."

She typed in Loretta's name and waited for the search results to populate. Several articles filled the screen. Mostly they were about the snow this winter, about an avalanche not far from here, and then there were more articles about Loretta.

"I guess they're having a funeral for Loretta in two days," she muttered. "They're expecting it to be big."

"As to be expected," Colton said. "Who's planning it?"

She skimmed the article, her eyes widening. "It looks like Yvonne is."

"Interesting. I guess that's why she came back into town early."

Sarah's gaze stopped at a quote from the story. "Colton, Yvonne is calling me out here in the article as Loretta's killer."

"What did she say?"

"That I should come forward. That Loretta trusted me, and I should be ashamed of myself for what I did. That it's my fault there's such a great loss to the medical community."

"You know none of that is true, right?"

Sarah nodded, knowing logically that Colton was right. But emotionally, the words felt like a stab to her heart. Even if she survived, how would she recover from this? Everyone thought she was a killer.

Maybe she had nothing to lose at this point. She needed to find answers now more than ever.

Colton wished he could snap his fingers and things would automatically right themselves. But he knew that couldn't happen. Though they'd made progress on this case, they still had so far to go.

Who had that man worked for? How was he involved in this? Colton still had so many questions that he wanted answers.

Behind him, Buzz let out a low whine and licked his paw.

"Sarah…?"

She leaned toward the dog. "What is it, boy?"

Buzz let out another whine when she touched his leg.

"Colton, there's a cut on his paw." Her voice tightened with worry. "It must have happened when we ran for the truck before the avalanche."

"How deep does it look?"

She cringed as she peered at the injury. "It looks pretty deep."

"See if there's anything in the glove compartment. Maybe we can wrap it."

She opened the door and pulled out a handkerchief. "This will work."

Carefully, she wrapped it around Buzz's paw. Within seconds, the cloth had turned red, though.

"We're going to have to take him to the vet, Sarah," Colton said.

"I agree," Sarah said. She couldn't stand the thought of the dog being in pain. "But Buzz is so identifiable. People will know who he is. They'll know who we are. How are we going to deal with that?"

"I'm not sure. But we don't have any other choice."

Sarah nodded. "I guess we'll just have to take that chance. He's risked his life for us more than once. Now it's our turn to help him."

TWENTY-SEVEN

Apprehension grew in Colton as they headed down the road. The man in the police car might be out of the picture right now, but someone else had been calling the shots. Whoever that person was, they were still faceless —and still a danger.

The man had mentioned a formula, which made Colton assume this had to do with the drug business. His thoughts immediately went to Yvonne.

It made sense for someone at a competing company to want to steal information. And Yvonne had the financial means to hire someone to help her get this proprietary formula. Maybe Yvonne had even planned for everything to happen while she was out of the country so she could have the perfect alibi.

Colton didn't know, but those things seemed like a good possibility.

"Sarah, I know this is going to sound crazy," Colton started, his mind snapping back to the present. "But I think we should take Buzz to his regular vet."

Her eyes widened before she quickly shook her head in disbelief. "Why would we do that?"

"Because it's another connection to Loretta. Maybe she talked to him."

"Loretta did love to talk about Buzz. And I did hear her mention the vet a few times. But it's so risky."

"At this point, everything is risky. I'm sure every cop within sixty miles of here is looking for us. It's only a matter of time, Sarah."

She frowned, a far-off look in her eyes. "If you really think that's what we should do, then let's do it. I trust you."

Instinctively, Sarah seemed to reach out and run her hand down Buzz's back. Fluffy pieces of hair floated in the air, but she didn't seem to notice.

Sarah's words did something to Colton's heart. *I trust you.* The two of them had come a long way over the past couple of days, Colton mused. Being thrown together in these circumstances had caused them to reevaluate everything, he supposed.

"What do you think of this, Buzz?" Sarah murmured.

The dog offered one affirmative bark.

"You like the idea?" she continued.

He barked again.

"I guess it's settled then." Sarah shrugged. "If Buzz is okay with it, then so am I."

Colton held back a smile. If only circumstances were different, this would be a memory to always hold close. "I guess so. You remember the vet's name?"

"It's Devon Kellogg. I even know where his office his. I went there once. Nice man."

"Great. Let's go."

Sarah directed him on how to get to the office. As Colton traveled, he kept his guard up, looking for anyone who might follow them.

He saw nothing.

But he couldn't relax yet. If any law enforcement saw them, they'd be done.

Colton wasn't ready to face that. No, they needed more

answers first. Because whoever was behind this had resources. He had no doubt this person would do everything within his or her power to frame Sarah for Loretta's murder.

He couldn't stomach the thought of Sarah being behind bars, and he would risk everything to stop that from happening.

Fifteen minutes later, they pulled up to a little brick office building that sat on the corner of a secondary road. Behind the vet's office was a gas station and then a grocery store stretched at the back of the lot. At least it was partially secluded here. He was thankful for that.

"What now?" Sarah asked, turning toward him in the truck.

Colton glanced at his watch. "It's lunchtime now. Do you think they close for lunch?"

She studied the area around them and shrugged. "I don't know. There aren't that many cars in the parking lot right now. Maybe that's a good sign."

As if on cue, a woman in scrubs stepped from a back door and climbed in her car.

"Any idea how many office workers he has?" Colton asked, trying to get a feel for the office.

"It's a small practice. Loretta liked it that way. When I came here with her once, the only people I remember are the receptionist and the doctor. I can't say for sure that's accurate, though."

"I think I should go inside with Buzz first," Colton said. "I'll be less recognizable with the dog."

"What about me?"

"Give it a few minutes and then come in. Keep your hat and sunglasses on. Make sure you wear the coat. It covers up some of your frame."

Sarah nodded, but the action made her look nervous. "Okay. Got it."

Colton took Buzz's leash, hoping this risk paid off. "Let's do this, boy."

Carefully, he helped the dog out, and he prayed for the best.

Sarah couldn't stop reliving the images of the avalanche covering that man's car. Though he'd tried to kill them, it still startled her to think about dying in that manner.

It also startled her to think about the fact that she, Colton and Buzz could have easily died that way also. If it hadn't been for Colton's quick thinking, none of them would be here right now.

Sarah always felt so safe when Colton was around. She deeply appreciated his involvement right now. She literally wouldn't have survived without him.

But as she stared at the door leading into the vet's office, a tingle of worry crept in.

A bad feeling lingered in her gut. Certainly Dr. Kellogg would recognize Buzz. He'd probably feel inclined to call the cops, whether he believed their story or not.

And then what would they do?

Sarah had no idea. But she wasn't ready to go to jail yet. She had to make something of her life first. Redeem her mistakes. End the pattern of sorrow her parents had laid out. It couldn't be too late for that.

Please, God...

She waited for five minutes before climbing from the truck. Tugging her hat down lower, she glanced around. She didn't see any cops or people watching her. That was a good sign. Maybe that meant that things were going smoothly inside so far. She hoped they would continue.

Sarah pulled the front door open and paused. Colton sat in the waiting area with Buzz lying at his feet. No one else was around.

She slipped into the seat beside him and whispered, "What's going on?"

"The vet just stuck his head out and said he'd be a minute," Colton whispered back. "That's all."

Anxiety continued to build. Dr. Kellogg hadn't seen Buzz yet. It was the calm before the storm.

Just then, Dr. Kellogg stepped out from the hallway, a big smile on his face. The man was probably in his fifties, but his hair was already white and matched his full mustache. The doctor was tall and thin and friendly.

"I'm afraid we're closed for lunch right now," he said pausing in front of them, his hands pressed together. He glanced at Buzz who wagged his tail at the sight of the doctor. "What's going on?"

Colton cleared his throat. "Our dog cut his foot. He's bleeding."

The doctor's eyes narrowed as he gazed at Buzz. He squatted down in front of the canine and picked up his paw. "Yes, you did hurt your foot, didn't you?"

"We're just worried that it won't heal correctly," Colton said.

"I understand." He rose. "You know what? I'll squeeze you guys in. Let me just get the room ready." He stepped back down the hallway.

But Sarah's warning bells were going off. He'd recognized Buzz, hadn't he? The doctor wasn't getting the room ready. No, he was probably calling the cops.

Before she could second-guess herself, Sarah stepped down the hallway and nudged the door open an inch or two. Sure enough, the doctor had his phone in his hand and had begun dialing.

"Wait," she said, stepping into the room. "Please, don't."

Dr. Kellogg's eyes widened, and he lowered the phone.

Realization washed over his features. "I almost didn't recognize you, Sarah."

"That's me."

His grim frown was all the answer she needed.

"A lot of people are looking for you right now," he said.

"I know. And I know why they're looking for me. But I
would have never hurt Loretta. In fact, I'm trying to protect Buzz and figure out who did this."

"Protect Buzz?"

Sarah nodded. "The real killer has been chasing us. He
thinks we have something that used to belong to Loretta.
But I don't. But he's willing to hurt us to get what he wants.
That's how Buzz was injured."

Dr. Kellogg observed her for a minute before nodding
slowly. "Loretta always spoke highly of you, you know."

"That's what I heard. I was…surprised." There was no
need to skirt around the truth.

"She liked for people to be scared of her initially. After
time, she would get softer." He smiled.

"I guess we didn't have enough time then."

"No, you didn't." His grin faded. "I was really sorry to
hear what happened to her."

She swallowed hard. "Me too. Look, I know it's weird
that I came here. But I'm desperate for answers, and Buzz
truly does need help. I thought you might have talked to
Loretta. That you might know something that could help
us find her killer."

"What are you looking for?" He crossed his arms, phone
still in hand, but then shook his head. "You know what?
Bring Buzz in here. Let me look at him. And we can talk
while I do that."

Sarah stepped into the hallway and motioned for Colton
and Buzz to join her. A minute later, they all squeezed

into the examination room, and Dr. Kellogg checked out Buzz's paw.

"I don't know what to tell you about Loretta," Dr. Kellogg started. "She didn't tell me anything too personal. Most of our conversations were about Buzz."

"When was the last time you saw her?" Colton asked. "I know Sarah said she brought Buzz in once. I'm talking before that."

"She came in about two months ago. Brought someone with her. I guess she hadn't hired you yet back then."

Sarah's breath caught. "Do you remember who she brought with her to help? She had trouble going out with Buzz in her wheelchair alone."

His lips twisted in thought. "I believe she said it was her landscaper."

Sarah and Colton exchanged a look.

"Frank?" Sarah asked. "Frank Mills?"

The doctor nodded, his eyes lighting up with recognition. "Yes, that sounds right."

Was that the connection they'd been looking for? Had Frank known more than they ever suspected?

"Why did Loretta come in?" Sarah asked. "For a normal checkup?"

"No, she actually wanted to update Buzz's microchip."

Everything began falling in place in Sarah's mind, but she still needed confirmation. "A new one? Was something wrong with the old one?"

"She said she'd developed a new, more effective one herself. She asked me if I'd mind helping her with it. Normally, I'd say no to something like that. But this was Loretta, and I knew she was on the genius level as far as IQ. Since it was her request, I did it for her."

"Did she say why this one was more effective?" Colton asked.

"No, she didn't. But I trusted her."

Sarah rubbed Buzz's head. "Is that all she said?"

"It is. I didn't ask too many questions." He bandaged Buzz's foot and then stood. "He should be all better now."

"Thank you for your help," Sarah said.

He turned apologetic. "I'll pretend you weren't here. I'm headed out to lunch. But be gone when I get back. And find Loretta's killer, okay?"

"We will," Sarah said.

He smiled down at the dog. "Buzz is a great dog."

Dr. Kellogg slipped out the back door. Sarah and Colton waited a couple minutes before stepping into the lobby.

Colton turned toward her, excitement dancing in his eyes. "The formula. It's on the microchip. It all makes sense now."

"You're right. It does."

Just then, a shadow darted out from behind the front desk.

A shadow holding a gun.

Sarah looked up. It was Debbie Wilcox, the CFO of Loretta's company.

Based on the lasers shooting from her eyes, she was here on a mission.

TWENTY-EIGHT

Colton stepped in front of Sarah and Buzz.

"What are you doing here, Debbie?" he asked, more puzzle pieces clicking together in his mind.

Yvonne was never behind this, was she? No, it had been Debbie this whole time.

Gone was the placid woman in mourning from the office. In her place was someone with vengeance and greed in her eyes. Right now, her business suit looked disheveled, as did her hair, as she stood in front of them.

"I tried to call Tad." Debbie sounded breathless. "He didn't answer. That's when I heard about the avalanche."

"Tad?" Colton asked. "Was he your boyfriend?"

Tears welled in Debbie's eyes. "Yes, that's right. We were in this together. You...you killed him."

"That's not true," Colton said. "He fired his gun, which started the avalanche."

"If you hadn't made things so difficult..." she sneered.

"How have you been following us, Debbie?" Sarah asked. "Were you tracking us via Buzz's microchip?"

She let out a haughty laugh. "No, there's no GPS in the microchip. My life couldn't possibly be that easy."

"Then how?" Sarah asked.

"Well, at first it was your phone, then it was Buzz's collar. But you two were smarter than I'd assumed. Finally, we started to track Colton's phone."

"But my phone is untraceable. You might have been able to get a radius from the signal triangulation, but you shouldn't have been able to track my exact location."

She smiled again. "Everything is traceable when you have the right resources."

"But you didn't know the formula information was on the microchip until today, did you?" Colton asked.

"I had no idea until I just heard you saying that. I only knew that Loretta had given the formula to you, Sarah. If we could get to you, we could get the information we needed."

Sarah's eyes widened with surprise. "How did you know that she'd given it to me? I didn't even know that."

"I heard her say she had the utmost confidence that you would protect it with your life."

Sarah let out a soft laugh. "She was right. I would protect Buzz with my life."

Debbie sneered again. "It wasn't supposed to end this way."

"It doesn't have to end this way," Colton said, his voice placid.

Debbie sniffled and then straightened. "Actually, it does. It just took me a while to realize it. Give me the dog."

"No way," Sarah muttered.

Debbie smiled again. "Of course you're not going to do this the easy way. That dog was the perfect place for Loretta to hide the formula for that new drug she was working on."

Colton frowned. "That dog has a formula in his microchip that will make you a lot of money, in other words."

"Exactly." Debbie's nostrils flared. "I should have been helping her. Loretta asked me some questions about this drug, but she never told me exactly what she was working on. So I sneaked into her lab one day and found out."

"And then you wanted to steal it from her?" Colton's stomach churned at the thought of the lengths people would go to for wealth and notoriety.

"I deserved this. I helped her with so much. And then she decides to give half her money to her." She snarled at Sarah.

"How'd you know?" Sarah asked, holding on to Buzz's leash like a lifeline.

"I overheard Loretta on the phone talking about it. After I figured out that she was up to something, I decided to get creative and planted a few bugs here and there. With the help of Tad, of course." The satisfaction in her voice tapered into sadness.

"I don't care about the money," Sarah said. "It was never about that."

"Must be nice to live in that kind of world," Debbie said.

"What about Frank? Why did you kill him?" Colton asked, even though he thought he knew the answer.

"I tried to get information from him. I figured he knew. But he wouldn't talk. He knew what I'd done. I had no other choice."

"You're a heartless, cruel woman," Sarah said, a look of pure disgust on her face.

"I just want what rightfully should be mine."

"You won't get away with this." Sarah pulled Buzz back.

"We'll see about that. I just need to get the microchip from Buzz, and I'll be out of your way." Debbie patted her leg. "Come here, boy."

Buzz growled.

Debbie's scowl grew. "I said come here. Don't make me do this the hard way."

Sarah stepped in front of Buzz. "Over my dead body."

"Okay, if we have to do it that way." Debbie raised her gun again.

"No!" Colton shouted, panic racing through him. "It doesn't have to be like this."

Debbie sneered. "Oh, honey. I've thought of every way possible. Yes, it does. Nothing is going to stand in my way."

"Try Buzz one more time," Sarah said.

What was Sarah doing? Certainly she had a plan here. No way would she say something like that without a good reason.

Colton hoped.

Debbie eyed her a moment before tapping her leg, a touch of hesitation to her actions. "Come here, boy."

Just as Sarah released the leash, she clucked her tongue. It was some kind of signal, wasn't it?

When she did, Buzz hurled toward Debbie, teeth bared.

Debbie's eyes widened with fear. She raised her gun. Pulled the trigger.

But the gun misfired. Nothing happened.

Instead, Debbie raised her hands to protect herself and let out a scream.

Buzz pounced on her, pinning her to the ground.

Colton grabbed her gun. Buzz continued to hold her down, growling on top of her, as the doors flew open. Police flooded inside.

As Detective Manning from the Spokane Police Department stepped inside, he gave a nod to Colton. "Someone from the gas station spotted you both in the truck that was taken from the cabin fire. They called in the tip."

"I figured we were on borrowed time," Colton said.

Manning frowned. "I got the email you sent, explaining what was going on."

"As you'll find out, Sarah wasn't behind any of this. Debbie Wilcox was." Colton glanced at Sarah, who practically crumpled on a bench there in the waiting room. He wanted nothing more than to go and be with her right now.

Soon enough. First, he needed to wrap up some loose ends.

"We're going to have a lot of questions," Manning said.

"Of course," Colton said. "Listen, I need a minute with Sarah before all the craziness starts. Is that okay?"

"Take five."

Colton walked toward Sarah and touched her shoulder, trying to get her attention and pull her out of her daze. Her head snapped toward him and she darted to her feet. As soon as their gazes connected, she folded herself into Colton's arms.

"I'm so glad you're okay," Colton murmured, drinking in her scent and the softness of her skin.

"Me too."

Colton stepped back, everything suddenly abundantly clear. "Sarah, I'm sorry."

She blinked up at him, her eyes warm and full of love. "For what?"

"For letting you walk away." He wiped a hair off of her face, realizing what a fool he'd been not to go after her.

"You didn't let me. I just did it on my own and—"

Colton shook his head, desperate to stop Sarah before she put too much blame on herself. "No, I should have come after you. You were right—I was so wrapped up in my own problems and issues that I was only thinking about myself."

She rested her hands on his chest, and her lips tugged down in a frown. "You had every right to do so. I didn't realize that until now. Until I experienced what it was like to see someone die. To feel…responsible."

"Loretta's death wasn't your fault." He stroked her arms,

trying to reassure her. It would take a while for both of them to process everything that had just happened.

"I know." Her voice cracked. "But it felt like it was. It will feel like that for a while."

"I can help you through that, and maybe you can help me also."

Sarah smiled. "I would like that."

"But you were wrong about one thing." Colton pulled her even closer, never wanting to let go. He'd been such an idiot to wait this long to connect with Sarah again.

"What's that?" Sarah gazed up at him.

"I should have never turned my back on you. Your dad left and then your mom went to jail…all you needed was stability."

"It's definitely hard to trust people, to think they're going to want to stick around. My mind automatically wants to go to the worst places."

"I know." Colton cupped Sarah's face with his hands. "I'm so sorry. I would have done things differently if I knew then what I know now. I would have listened to you more. I would have tried harder."

"I should have dealt with my past so I wouldn't have had that knee-jerk reaction. I'm the one who should be apologizing."

"Oh, Sarah." Without saying anything else, Colton's lips met hers. This time, there wasn't any hesitation. It was just the joyous reunion of two people who'd loved and lost… and who'd found each other again.

Before their kiss ended, someone nuzzled between them.

Colton paused and looked down. It was Buzz.

He pulled away and laughed.

"Good job back there, boy." He patted the dog's head.

Buzz seemed to soak up the attention, a new light entering the dog's eyes. He knew this was over too, didn't he? Maybe the canine even knew that he'd saved the day.

Because Buzz *had* saved the day. They wouldn't be alive right now without him. And they would make sure he was treated like a king for the rest of his life.

TWENTY-NINE

A month after Loretta's killer had confessed to everything, including Tad's involvement, Sarah stood in front of Colton at a little church not far from Colton's cabin in North Idaho. The building was quaint, with stained glass windows, a white steeple and glossy wooden pews.

There weren't a lot of people here at the wedding, as per Sarah's wishes. But Colton's family had come in, as well as Sarah's sister and her family. Alfred Jennings and Yvonne were also in attendance. In recent weeks, the two had become friends.

Sarah hadn't wanted a big ceremony, no bridesmaids or groomsmen. But Buzz did sit on stage beside them, their wedding rings tucked into a holder on his collar.

Yes, Buzz had officially become a part of Sarah's family, as per Loretta's last wishes.

Shortly after Debbie Wilcox had been arrested, Sarah and Colton had met with Alfred Jennings, and he'd told them about the changes to Loretta's will, as well as how Loretta had felt strongly toward Sarah. Loretta truly had left that money to Sarah and said she viewed her almost like a daughter. He theorized that Loretta had left the cash in Buzz's bag because she'd feared someone would try to kill her. She wanted to make sure Buzz was taken care of.

The microchip had been obtained from Buzz. On it there were instructions from Loretta. Yvonne was to be given the proprietary formula for the new ALS drug she'd been working on. She'd known the formula would be in high demand. The new drug had apparently had great results in Loretta, and those closest to her had seen the changes.

She'd hidden the formula in the one safe place she could think of. Only Alfred Jennings knew the truth, but he hadn't been able to reveal the information until a month after her death. She wanted her will to be sorted out first.

Though Sarah had initially wondered if Yvonne was guilty in all of this, once she'd met the woman, she'd really liked her. She truly had been a friend to Loretta. Despite her tough words in that newspaper article concerning Sarah, she realized Yvonne had just acted out of loyalty to her friend.

Everything seemed to be falling in place.

Finally.

Because it had been a hard-fought battle to get to where she was today.

Sarah was going to continue with her art, working from a studio Colton had set up for her in his barn. He'd even added a heater for those cold winter days. A gallery in Coeur d'Alene had asked for several pieces of her work, and one of the potential buyers from the last art show she'd been to—right before Loretta died—had purchased one of Sarah's paintings.

As for the money Loretta left her…though Sarah had initially been tempted to give it back or refuse it, Colton had convinced her not to do that. Instead, she invested it in several nonprofits. One was for foster children. Another was for incarcerated women with children. The third was for a husky rescue group.

The rest...well, Sarah was considering starting her own gallery one day.

But for now, she just wanted to stay here with Colton and to explore how great life could be together. Colton had taken that job with the Idaho State Police after all. His healing had come full circle.

"Do you take this man to be your husband, to have and to hold, from this day forward?" the pastor asked.

Sarah smiled up at Colton, realizing she'd never loved someone as much as she loved him. Having him come back into her life was an answer to a prayer she hadn't realized she'd prayed.

"I do," she said, her voice unwavering.

"And do you take this woman to be your lawfully wedded wife?"

"I do." The same smile stretched across Colton's face, and love radiated from his gaze.

A few minutes later, Colton kissed the bride, and the two became man and wife.

Despite everything that had happened, good had finally come from it all. Sarah was forever grateful to have Colton by her side and to have found her safe place in his arms.

* * * * *

*If you enjoyed this exciting story of
suspense and romance, pick up these other stories
from Christy Barritt:*

Hidden Agenda
Mountain Hideaway
Dark Harbor
Shadow of Suspicion
The Baby Assignment
The Cradle Conspiracy

*Available now from Love Inspired Suspense!
Find more great reads at www.LoveInspired.com*

Dear Reader,

Thank you so much for reading *Trained to Defend*. I hope you enjoyed Sarah and Colton's story, as well as meeting Buzz.

I love animals. In fact, I have four dogs, and they're all different sizes, breeds and personalities. I always love being able to incorporate furry friends into my stories because my own dogs add so much love and adventure to my life.

In the book, Sarah talks about wanting a safe place to land. Do you ever feel like you need a safe place in your life? When things feel overwhelming, we all need somewhere we can go to rest and recharge.

Through the Bible, we know that God is our true safety. In hard times, He's who we can run to. When trouble hits, we can rest in the blessed assurance of God's promises. Let's never forget that we always have a safe place in Him.

Blessings,

AVAILABLE THIS MONTH FROM
Love Inspired Suspense

TRAINED TO DEFEND
K-9 Mountain Guardians • by Christy Barritt
Falsely accused of killing her boss, Sarah Peterson has no choice but
to rely on her ex-fiancé, former detective Colton Hawk, and her boss's
loyal husky for protection. But can they clear her name before the real
murderer manages to silence her for good?

AMISH COUNTRY KIDNAPPING
by Mary Alford
For Amish widow Rachel Albrecht, waking up to a man trying to kidnap
her is terrifying—but not as much as discovering he's already taken her
teenaged sister. But when her first love, *Englischer* deputy Noah Warren,
rescues her, can they manage to keep her and her sister alive?

SECRET MOUNTAIN HIDEOUT
by Terri Reed
A witness to murder, Ashley Willis hopes her fake identity will keep
her hidden in a remote mountain town—until she's tracked down by
the killer. Now she has two options: flee again...or allow Deputy Sheriff
Chase Fredrick to guard her.

LONE SURVIVOR
by Jill Elizabeth Nelson
Determined to connect with her last living family member, Karissa Landon
tracks down her cousin—and finds the woman dead and her son a
target. Now going on the run with her cousin's baby boy and firefighter
Hunter Raines may be the only way to survive.

DANGER IN THE DEEP
by Karen Kirst
Aquarium employee Olivia Smith doesn't know why someone wants
her dead—but her deceased husband's friend, Brady Johnson, knows a
secret that could explain it. Brady vowed he'd tell no one his friend had
been on the run from the mob. But could telling Olivia save her life?

COLORADO MANHUNT
by Lisa Phillips and Jenna Night
The hunt for fugitives turns deadly in these two thrilling novellas, where
a US marshal must keep a witness safe after the brother she testified
against escapes prison, and a bounty hunter discovers she and the
vicious gang after her bail jumper tracked the man's twin instead.

**LOOK FOR THESE AND OTHER LOVE INSPIRED BOOKS WHEREVER
BOOKS ARE SOLD, INCLUDING MOST BOOKSTORES, SUPERMARKETS,
DISCOUNT STORES AND DRUGSTORES.**

LISATM0120

COMING NEXT MONTH FROM
Love Inspired Suspense

Available February 4, 2020

MOUNTAIN HOSTAGE
K-9 Mountain Guardians • by Hope White

After an ambush during a hike through the mountains, Zoe Pratt ends up injured and her friend kidnapped. Now Zoe's a target...and relying on search and rescue volunteer Jack Monroe and his K-9 partner is her only shot at survival.

AMISH COUNTRY UNDERCOVER
by Katy Lee

Taking the reins of her father's Amish horse-trading business, Grace Miller's prepared for backlash over breaking community norms—but not for sabotage. Now someone's willing to do anything it takes to make sure she fails, and it's undercover FBI agent Jack Kaufman's mission to stop them.

RUNAWAY WITNESS
Protected Identities • by Maggie K. Black

On the run after a security breach of the witness protection program leaves her exposed, Iris James trusts nobody—until the undercover detective she thought was dead comes to her rescue. With a killer's henchmen on their trail, can Mack Gray keep her alive long enough to testify?

COLD CASE CONNECTION
Roughwater Ranch Cowboys • by Dana Mentink

Private investigator Sergio Ross is determined to catch his sister's killer. But with all the clues hinting at a connection to another cold case murder, he has to work with Helen Pike—a woman linked to both deaths—to get justice before they become the next victims.

KILLER INSIGHT
Covert Operatives • by Virginia Vaughan

Convinced his brother isn't the Back Roads Killer as the police believe, single dad Bryce Tippett asks FBI agent Lucy Sanderson to create a profile of the killer. But when someone begins stalking Lucy just as she arrives in town, can Bryce ensure she lives to reveal the truth?

SAFE HOUSE UNDER FIRE
by Elisabeth Rees

Bank clerk Lilly Olsen is the only witness who can identify a vicious con man—and he'll kill her *and* her teenage daughter to silence her. FBI agent David McQueen will guard them with his life. But can he succeed when the criminal inexplicably keeps finding their safe houses?

LOOK FOR THESE AND OTHER LOVE INSPIRED BOOKS WHEREVER BOOKS ARE SOLD, INCLUDING MOST BOOKSTORES, SUPERMARKETS, DISCOUNT STORES AND DRUGSTORES.

LISCNM0120